The Scent of Ginger

by RK Raker

Cover photograph of Yellow Ginger flower by Bradley Wong

V2

ISBN-13: 978-1494880415
ISBN-10: 1494880415

The footnotes are for the benefit of readers unfamiliar with non-English words and phrases commonly used by locals in Hawaii. These Hawaiian, pidgin, Korean, Japanese and Chinese words are included in the story out of respect for the multicultural heritage of the islands.

Dedicated to "Paddleboard" Bob, may the adventures continue...

Chapter 1

The flowerbed footing the perimeter wall of the residence was overflowing with hundreds of tropical flowers, but it was the sticky sweet scent of Ginger that forced him to cover his nose. The fragrance assaulted his senses. It didn't mix well with his aftershave.

Detective Morimoto stepped through the front gate of the Kahala mansion knowing what to expect. He was going through the motions to satisfy the brass and higher-ups. They were pushing hard for some kind of breakthrough. He knew there would be no fingerprints, no footprints, no eye-witnesses, no video surveillance or any useful trace evidence. The morning would be wasted interviewing gardeners and servants, and trying to get a list of the stolen items from the house owners, who, of course, were away on a ski vacation in Montana. He had decided to delegate most of this work to the rookies in his department. The final report, however, would have to come from him, so here he was.

As soon as he had walked down the palm tree-lined driveway and spotted the blacked out video cameras and motion detectors, he knew it was the damn Mongoose. The carefully cut hole in the side window, the point of entry, confirmed his judgment. This was the 16th burglary that fit the Mongoose' MO in the last ten years—the third in the last six months.

The Mongoose is ramping up.

He found this fact interesting and noteworthy, but not particularly useful. The thief was smart and successful. Morimoto knew that success bred confidence and more brazen behavior. The increased activity was just that, more activity, more messes to trudge through, more work.

Perhaps he would make a mistake, Morimoto thought just before he entered the foyer. *Wishful thinking—it never helped before.*

He kicked the driveway sand off his Gucci loafers, made sure his Tommy Bahama Aloha shirt was tucked-in and that his slacks were still perfectly creased. Once inside, he looked at the sharp figure in the full-length mirror hanging to the left of the massive oak doors. He imagined the owners of the mansion pruning themselves before jetting off for their vacation. He saw himself standing next to them, taller, better looking.

The mirror doesn't lie.

He raked his thinning black hair into place and admired the shine of his Cordovan leather shoes, the line of his stone grey Armani blazer, and the slight bulge of his shoulder holster.

Damn, this black belt looks great, he thought, then looking lower, *and there will be an extra bulge for my sweet baby later.*

"Suzuki," he yelled. "Give me a rundown. Then start with the gardeners—neighbors— see if anyone's home."

Morimoto listened to Suzuki's report and asked a few curt questions while making his way through the house. He took everything in, but wasn't really interested.

The huge marble columned house had been hit just a few hours before dawn. It was owned by one of the many multimillionaire old-money families that ruled the island— the Dillinghams. Just like the other fifteen homes, the family had recently been in the news for making a massive real estate development deal where they stood to profit in the hundreds of millions. This time, the once untouchable Sandy Beach preservation zone, under the Dillingham's care since the overthrow of the Hawaiian Monarchy, had succumbed to the pressure of progress and greed. A Japanese conglomerate planned a mega-resort on the property.

Morimoto could care less, but the connection was not lost on him—more than burglary motivated the Mongoose. He didn't just steal from the islands' wealthiest families, he tried to hurt them by destroying their innermost sanctums. The Mongoose wanted them to feel vulnerable. Some houses had even been hit more than once. Morimoto was no Hawaiian homelands expert, but he, and others, suspected that the level of ransacking was some kind of bizarre type of punishment or revenge for participating in the development of Hawaiian land.

They paved paradise, and put up a parking lot, and all that crap, he thought.

Morimoto's eyes adjusted quickly to the dimly lit interior of the house. He was immediately taken aback by the total destruction. He always was. He didn't understand it. It did not fit within his tightly controlled world. Morimoto could wrap his brain around the burglary, the lifting of jewelry, silver settings, priceless paintings, Hawaiian artifacts and other valuable loot, but the typhoon-like ransacking of every major room in the mansion was— *strange, weird, unnecessary, psychotic, over-the-top.* He could think of a hundred words to describe the chaos left behind, but nothing did justice to the actual scene.

Today was no exception. In fact, it looked as if this time the Mongoose had been particularly agitated or intent on creating maximum destruction. Everything in sight was broken, smashed, slashed, ripped, torn, toppled and tossed about. Not one piece of furniture, fixture, knickknack, painting, or heirloom had escaped the Mongoose's wrath. He had done a thorough job. Even the Koa wood floors and freshly painted walls were defaced. Morimoto wondered what kind of drugs drove this maniac into such frenzy. It

3

made him tired just thinking about it. The expenditure of emotion and energy required to do such damage seemed out of place, alien, to him. It just made his job that much more difficult.

Damn, what a mess.

Morimoto took his obligatory notes, shouted a few more orders and left the crime scene. He stopped by his apartment in Makiki for a quick few lines and a good-morning squeeze from his new girlfriend—he needed something to get him through another day.

Chapter 2

Lou sat in the back of the dimly lit bar scanning the few remaining patrons and watching the front entrance. It had been a busy Friday night at Sandy's. His table was dirty with crumbs and grease, and wet from spilled drinks. The floor was sticky. His boots made squishy sounds as he shifted his weight on the cracked leather chair. The air was stale with the stench of cigarettes, burnt Korean BBQ, *kimchi*[1] and tequila. He sipped his gin and tonic.

The top-notch girls had already gone home. Only two dancers were still working the stage, one Filipina and the other Japanese. Both were in various stages of undress as they gyrated slowly to the hip-hop beat. Neither seemed very motivated, they were just going through the motions. It was almost closing time. The few men scattered on each end of the stage were not that energetic either. They were running out of dollar bills. They seemed content to slouch over their drinks, only halfheartedly encouraging the girls to come closer and reveal more.

Another hostess came by, again offering to sit with him or bring some *Pupus*[2] to the table. He knew it would be more natural if he let the older woman sit with him and order a twenty-dollar drink, but he just wasn't in the mood to make conversation. Instead, he ordered another gin and tonic and gave her a ten-dollar tip. This seemed to satisfy her and he was left alone in the smoky darkness.

"I don't see him," the clear voice said in his head.

"What about the guy in the far corner getting a private lap dance?" he whispered.

---

[1] Korean pickles
[2] Appetizers

"Nope, too short and stocky," the reply came back immediately. "Also, he's Japanese national, were looking for a Polynesian."

"I know what we're looking for," he said, slightly irritated.

"Hey Lou, don't get so touchy."

"Well, I'm not the one relaxing in my bed with the benefit of night vision, face recognition, infrared and who the hell knows what," he said. "Just answer my questions and give me new information. I don't need the commentary."

"Okey-dokey," the voice responded. "Someone's a little bit on edge tonight."

"Speak for yourself."

He finished his drink.

"I think I'll call it a night."

Lou needed some sleep. It had been a long day. His regular job as a security consultant for the governor's office was keeping him busy. An election year was coming up, so he had even more to look forward to. As it was, he easily put in sixty hours a week and had not had a two-day weekend in six months. This gig, though more of a hobby than a job, was starting to add to his stress level.

"Stay where you are, I just picked up a likely suspect about a block away, heading in your direction."

"Roger that."

A few minutes later, a large Polynesian man walked into the bar. He was at least six feet tall and built like a linebacker. He was clean-shaven, with light brown skin. He had Maori tattoos on his neck and right arm. He was dressed neatly in a short-sleeved collared Aloha shirt and pressed khaki pants. He walked up to the bar with confidence. His open toed sandals made flip-flop sounds as the leather soles stuck to the floor and then slapped his heels. He took a stool and ordered a Bourbon on the rocks.

"That's him," the voice said.

"Hundred percent?" Lou asked.

"Running final facial recognition scan now."

From his vantage point in the rear of the bar, he watched the Polynesian man's eyes. They took in everything. His movements were deliberate, calculated. He looked through the smoke filled air towards the back of the bar where Lou was sitting. His gaze paused for a moment, focusing on the *haole*[3] sipping his gin and tonic, but then continued with his assessment of the establishment.

"This one's careful," the voice said.

"Looks like it."

"Okay, results are back. This is definitely our guy."

Lou threw a couple of bucks on the table and took the back exit out of Sandy's. He crossed the alley and found a position in the shadows. He waited.

"Do you want me to call for backup?"

"No, I can do this on my own tonight," Lou replied.

"You sure? He looks like a pretty big *moke*,[4]" the voice said.

Lou laughed at his partner's attempt to sound local.

"You know I don't like repeating myself," Lou said. "Especially when it's after three o'clock in the morning and I'm crouching in the shadows of a urine-filled back alley."

"Yep, I had to turn off the scent receptors. I feel for you *braddah*."

"Thanks for the empathy. You can cut the *pidgin*.[5]"

A hurt silence settled over the alleyway. Lou felt bad about taking his sour mood out on his friend.

"How about some music?" He asked.

"Hotel California, coming right up."

---

[3] White foreigner
[4] Rough local boy
[5] Local Hawaiian dialect

Almost immediately, the soft country rock rhythms of the Eagles' 1970s classic were playing in the background. It was not exactly what Lou had in mind, but it did match the mood of the evening. Lou, long-term memory impaired, preferred more recent and independent artists, while his friend and partner James, the voice in his head that remembered everything, was still stuck in the 70s and 80s.

Even after all of this time Lou was still amazed at the feeling of having a voice or music piped directly through his brain. He would have difficulty explaining it to someone else if he had to. Luckily, very few people knew about this special arrangement. The voice communication functionality was easy to accept, it was just like talking on a high quality headset and cell phone—except there was no visible equipment and his ears still heard everything around him.

The piped-in music, however, was a completely different level of involvement. It emanated from a unique place deep inside his brain, and spread out encompassing his entire consciousness. The sound completely enveloped him, yet he remained in control of the volume. All of his instincts, intellect and senses remained fully functional. He still heard the soft chatter in the parking lot and the cars passing by on the main street, but the rhythms of the music surrounded him in a quadraphonic, no, a "holistic-phonic" experience.

Lou wondered what the great composers and musicians would've thought if they could have experienced their music at this level. It would have surely blown their minds. Perhaps they did. Maybe that's why so many great musicians went insane.

The seconds ticked by slowly. Lou hated to wait. Unfortunately, it seemed like 80% of the time when he was out on a mission, that's all he did—wait. He used the time to survey the layout, strengthen his Ki^6 and store his adrenaline.

---

[6] Inner strength

The alley, crowded with overflowing garbage cans, cardboard boxes, and recycle bins, led to a parking lot a block over. It was dark except for a few naked bulbs hanging over the back exits of the strip mall of bars and restaurants lining the south side of Keeaumoku Street. Only a few cars were still cruising the main street at this time of night. The sidewalks, busy earlier in the evening, were empty except for a few late-night patrons making their way home. A homeless man slept about fifty paces further down the alley in the corner of an alcove between Sandy's and Thai House, a popular karaoke bar. It was relatively quiet.

The glow from the neon lights fronting Sandy's switched off. It was closing time. The bouncer and bartender ushered out the few customers that hung on until the last drink of the night. He heard the front door close and lock.

"Not long now," Lou whispered to himself.

A few minutes later, the Polynesian man entered the front of the alley and quickly stepped in to the shadows.

"You got him?" the voice asked.

"Yep, any weapons?"

"A switchblade in his back pocket, nothing else that I can see."

"Copy that."

Lou felt for the stun gun clipped to the side of his belt. He sometimes carried a Glock 26, but this guy was a predator of women, a low-life rapist, a gun was not needed. The stun gun and his hands and fists would be sufficient, and more satisfactory. He would punish the man a little bit, just to send a message to any other would be rapists in the state. Lou looked forward to that, but remained mindful of his goal. Capture the perpetrator in the act and bring him to justice, not kill.

The workers from Sandy's slowly started to exit the back door. Some headed to the parking lot, while others made for the main street hailing taxicabs or rides with friends. Lou kept his eyes out for the Filipino dancer. This was the perp's preferred target and MO. Six exotic dancers, all young Filipino girls, had been kidnapped and raped over the last four months in the Keeaumoku Red-light district. The police had a vague description of the man, but they hadn't been able to identify or apprehend him.

"The Voice," which Lou sometimes liked to call his partner James, with his powerful computers, surveillance systems, and unlimited public and private database access, had been able to pin point the rapist. Honolulu Police Department (HPD) had been notified, but statewide budget cuts didn't allow for a rapist of exotic dancers to be placed high on the most wanted list. The city's Police Department was grappling with many other priorities. They were, however, happy to have Lou's assistance.

The girl left the bar and walked towards the parking lot. Lou moved deeper into the shadows as she passed by. He stood perfectly still, waiting to see if the Polynesian man would make his move.

He did.

Chapter 3

James, "the Voice" in Lou's head, saw, heard, felt and tasted everything that happened in the next few minutes. Only the sense of smell was lacking, James had purposely left the olfactory receptors turned off. He thoroughly enjoyed experiencing the world Lou brought to his extrasensory holographic control room, but he appreciated it even more when he could selectively filter out or enhance specific characteristics of the scene. The smell of urine and rotting garbage were not necessary to comprehend the unfolding situation.

He maximized all of his recording, analysis, surveillance and experiential equipment. Every sensory connection was primed. The backlights in his room and the numerous monitors automatically dimmed. The LED grid lines along the floor, walls and ceilings vibrated, bringing the 3-D scene to life. He was now completely immersed in Lou's world. He was there. The feeling was slightly uncomfortable, but it was also thrilling. He loved the sensation of being there with Lou, bringing justice to the darker corners of the city.

The Polynesian man, which by now James had identified as 32-year-old Tongan, Jesse Fua'taola, let the Filipino dancer pass and then carefully stepped in behind her. He kept a respectable distance so as not to alarm his prey.

They passed Lou on their way to the parking lot. Lou and James were both amazed at the oblivious nature of the young girl.

Hadn't she heard that there was a kidnapper and rapist in the neighborhood?

She walked slowly, almost absentmindedly, towards her car. Her flimsy white, one-piece barely covered her five-foot frame. She smoked a long-filtered cigarette, took a drag and stubbed her five-inch heels into a grease-filled pothole.

Lou smelled the menthol and her cheap perfume. James heard her curse as she nearly toppled over.

Apparently, she had difficulty doing two things at once.

The Polynesian man on the other hand, moved silently and steadily, and at just the right pace. He would be directly behind her when she reached the parking lot. Lou stayed close, but kept to the shadows.

The dancer entered the parking lot and reached into her purse, teetering precariously on her heels. She pulled out the keys for her shiny white Nissan and the front lights blinked in response. The man took out his stiletto and sprang into action, coming up quickly behind her. Lou didn't believe he would stab the girl, the knife was just a way to scare and subdue his victim. Nevertheless, Lou determined it would be safer for all involved if he intercepted the criminal before he got his arms around her.

"Better move now," James said.

Lou grunted an obscenity in response.

He was already a few steps behind the Polynesian man. He had his stun gun, a military-grade Air-Taser, charged, poised, and ready to go. One burst, 500,000 volts, and the 200+ pounder would be rendered helpless, withering on the gravel parking lot.

Bishh-Zap! The taser's electrode darts flew through the air, connecting with Fua'taola's lower back.

Click click click, electricity pulsed through the thin wires.

The man's legs went limp, but he didn't go to the ground. Lou retrieved the stiletto with one quick motion, knocked his legs sideways and threw him down. The Polynesian man turned his head just in time to see Lou grinning before he hit the gravel hard.

The girl screamed.

"Shush, it's okay. I'm with HPD."

Lou flashed a fake badge. He lied, but he found that it was easier that way. The victims calmed down faster if they thought it was a cop and perps cooperated more readily if they thought he was the law. Lou looked around, and then gave the man one more burst before he removed the electrodes.

"No one in the vicinity," James said.

"Okay."

Lou cuffed the man. Then he rolled him over so he could see his face. He wanted to look the rapist in the eye before he pummeled him a few times.

"I'm calling 911 now," James said.

"Okay," Lou said. "You don't have to watch this part."

James didn't approve of the excessive use of force and beatings that Lou often gave to his catch. It was a dark side of his friend that he didn't completely understand. The behavior was clearly a byproduct of his special operations training and deployment experience.

They rarely discussed Lou's tours of duty in Iraq and Afghanistan. That was part of his friend's life that was still closed and not open for analysis. So James was forced to accept the idea that his partner needed to expel his aggression, frustration and disgust in some way, at least this outlet was productive and the recipient almost always deserved it. James usually protested slightly, but then made sure the recordings were erased and that any physical evidence was rendered useless before zealous defense attorneys could make a case against his friend.

"Understood. What about the girl?"

"She can watch or she can go. It's up to you," Lou said.

"We don't need her. HPD has enough hard evidence to make their case. Cut her loose."

"Get out of here," Lou said to the dancer.

She didn't need to be told twice. She hopped into her Nissan and sped out of the parking lot.

Lou bound the man's legs with a plastic tie. He stood over the Polynesian man and waited until he came around. He took a pair of black leather gloves out of his back pocket.

That was James' cue.

"Lou, you don't have to," he said.

"You're wrong, James."

James didn't say anything further. He switched off the auditory and kinetic receptors. He minimized the holographic grid and sent the remaining transmission to a small LED screen in the corner of the room. He left the optical sensors and local surveillance systems on, but he averted his attention to other tasks. He didn't have the stomach to watch, but just in case something went awry he allowed the recording to continue.

James began to compile the evidence he had against the perpetrator and started the summary report he would submit to HPD in the next few hours. He felt confident that this would be a slam-dunk—another low-life off the streets.

A few minutes later, out of the corner of his eye, he noticed the LED screen flicker. It flashed with snowy contrast and then went dark. James immediately switched the transmission to his primary console.

The connection had been broken.

James was flying completely blind. No data was coming in from Lou.

He switched to his back-up systems. He ran emergency diagnostics. There still was no transmission from Lou. This was highly irregular. Their connection could only be severed by both of them saying the encrypted password within thirty seconds of each other, or if Lou was unconscious—he certainly wasn't taking a nap.

James became alarmed. His heart rate monitor beeped a warning. His ventilator fought to keep his breathing regular. The bed sheets soaked up his beads of sweat.

He checked for any video cameras in the vicinity. One security camera outside the 7-Eleven had a partial view of the parking lot. He enhanced the video and zoomed in to where his partner had last been observed.

HPD had not arrived yet. Lou was nowhere in sight. James thought he could make out the perp lying on the ground.

Everything else looked quiet.

Chapter 4

Lou didn't notice the white van pull into the parking lot. Its lights were off and it moved in slowly behind him. He was focused on inflicting maximum pain.

"Fua'taola, your days of robbing and raping are over."

"Who the fuck are you? You got no right," the Polynesian man replied wincing in pain.

Lou knew all the right pressure points throughout the body. He was an expert at the hard and soft techniques of *Sin Moo Hapkido*,[7] the Ying and Yang of combat and life. He could take most common objects and turn them into deadly weapons, but he didn't need any additional tools to complete his current job—the stun gun had done the trick. He could subdue a sumo wrestler with one thumb pressed into the correct meridian. He could have snapped any bone in this man's body with the flick of a wrist or a quick chop from the palm of his hand. Lou's kicks and punches were lethal, but he preferred grasping, pulling, pushing, and taking advantage of his opponents negative energy. This man had an abundant supply. Lou's gloved hands itched for action.

Fua'taola screamed as Lou found a particularly sensitive pressure point near his pelvis.

"Can-it," Lou whispered in the man's ear. "You still feel like wrestling with that little Filipino girl?"

The subdued man shook his head.

Lou moved his right thumb to another pressure point, just below the thigh.

"This is going to hurt —probably will walk with a limp for a while. But, hey, you'll still be able to pace your prison cell."

The man screamed again.

---

[7] A style of Korean martial arts

Lou smiled.

He was relaxed, calm, in no way angry or agitated. Lou had practiced the Korean martial art of Sin Moo Hapkido over several decades and had recently earned the title of grandmaster. He had studied under Ji Han-Jae, the founder of the discipline, in Seoul and in the US. Lou remembered the words his teacher had told him when as a third year student he had asked about the meaning of the words, Sin Moo Hapkido.

Master Han had replied, "*Sin* means higher mind or higher spirit, and *Moo* refers to the martial arts."

Lou adjusted his position.

"*Hap* means bringing together or harmonizing," his teacher had explained. "*Ki* is the energy that connects the mind and the body, and *Do* is the way this happens."

Fua'taola groaned.

Lou pushed harder trying to find the harmony in the situation.

Sin Moo Hapkido, he remembered his teachers say. *It's a way of using martial arts to harmonize the mind and body in order to reach a higher more enlightened state of existence.*

Lou followed the philosophy of his master teacher faithfully, but like any man he had his share of weaknesses. He didn't think his teacher would approve of his current actions. Inflicting pain for the purpose of punishment, revenge, or some misguided sense of justice had no place in master Han's teachings and it probably didn't move him along the path of enlightenment, but it felt satisfying.

Lou punched the man in the face a couple of times. Blood gushed from his nose and swollen lips.

"It hurts now, but I expect you'll feel worse in a few days," Lou said, bending over the man.

18

The Polynesian man shook his head, pleading for mercy. Suddenly, a lead pipe smashed into the back of Lou's skull. He lost consciousness immediately. The three men wearing black clothes, black ski masks, black baseball caps and black gloves, lifted Lou off the Polynesian man and threw him into the van.

The door slammed and they sped away into the night.

Chapter 5

"This is Doctor James Spencer, please connect me with Detective Morimoto."

"It's nearly four o'clock in the morning Sir, Detective Morimoto doesn't start his shift until 8 AM," the dispatcher said.

"This is an emergency," James tried to stay calm. He knew that getting angry or overly aggressive would not help the situation.

"I know the Detective well. We have worked together on many occasions. I'm sure he won't mind if you just send him a page or a text. Please just give him my name and number and tell him that it's urgent."

"I've heard of you and your work with the HPD, Mister Spencer. I'll send the Detective a text."

"Thank you."

James closed Skype and opened his "To Do" notepad. He dictated the following message and moved it to the top of his list.

Get Morimoto's cell and pager number!!!

Still limited to the 7-Eleven video camera, James watched as the police officers discussed what to do with the Polynesian man lying in the parking lot. The EMS medics arrived, lifted the man up and checked him out in the back of the ambulance.

"Damn, I wish I had audio."

He sent the feed from the 7-Eleven to a secondary monitor. He opened his visual analytics software and gave the system a few short commands.

"Rewind to 02:00 hours. Play-back at half speed. If any automobiles or people appear in the frame, queue-up the footage and ping me."

He wanted to determine exactly who had been in the parking lot just prior to and during the disappearance of Lou. In the meantime, he monitored the police scanner to see if he could hear what was going on with the perp and the police officers. It looked like they were about to cut his wrist bands and set him loose.

"There has to be a way to communicate with these guys," he said. James had the habit of talking to himself. It helped him think.

Then it occurred to him. It would be highly irregular and definitely illegal, but these were special circumstances.

James quickly logged on to the HPD intranet and hacked into the dispatchers system. He located his original 911 call and the dispatcher's instructions to the patrol cars. He noted the car numbers and the officers' names. He configured his personal microphone to sound like a local female and took over a vacant dispatch station/CPU. He called the patrol car closest to where the officers were standing.

"Car 116, Officer Yoshinaga, please acknowledge."

James repeated the request.

"Yoshinaga here," the patrol officer replied.

"This is Janice, Dispatch 017, I'm going to connect you with Doctor James Spencer. He's a consultant with the HPD and called in the original 911. Standby, please," James said.

"10-4"

James canceled the female voice and set his microphone to normal.

"Officer Yoshinaga, this is James Spencer. Thanks for taking my call."

"How can I help you sir?"

"The Polynesian man is the prime suspect for the Keeaumoku kidnappings and rapes—Jesse Fua'taola. Please bring him in for questioning. Detective Morimoto will be interrogating him in the morning," James said.

"What happened here?" Yoshinaga asked.

It felt strange trying to explain to the officer what was going on. James usually relied on Lou and his excellent rapport with HPD to tie up the loose ends after a successful mission. Lou was the front man. He was more comfortable being "the voice" in Lou's head. He remained behind the scenes, doing the analysis, searches, reports—orchestrating the show from a distance. He rarely made direct contact with people outside of his trusted inner circle of friends, colleagues and caregivers. Occasionally he joined in conference calls or meetings as the "talking head" on a smartphone or video screen, but he preferred to listen, rather than talk. When he was required to verbalize his thoughts, he had difficulty stringing more than a few phrases together at a time. His ventilator forced him to breathe every five or six seconds, making his attempts at speaking choppy and phrasal.

"The premises must be secured. There may be evidence of an additional kidnapping. I have reason to believe...that Lou Costelilia was assaulted and abducted after apprehending the suspect."

"Will do, sir. Anything else?"

Officer Yoshinaga was polite and professional, but he didn't sound very happy about suddenly being pulled into a crime scene. A simple arrest would have been more to his liking, especially at the end of his ten-hour shift.

"One more thing, please ask the suspect if he saw or heard anyone or anything other than Lou Costelilia in the parking lot. He may have seen what happened."

"10-4 and out," the patrol officer said.

James switched to the live feed from the 7-Eleven. The ambulance left the scene and he watched as the officers taped off the area and went through the motions of questioning the suspect. A few minutes later, Officer Yoshinaga drove off with the Keeaumoku rapist, presumably taking him to HPD headquarters. James doubted Fua'taola had heard or seen anything useful. He would check back with the patrol officer later. The 7-Eleven footage was his best bet in determining what happened.

He had already received several pings from the secondary computer system. He ordered the primary system to stay active, but fade to the background. James brought the 7-Eleven images to the forefront. He began scanning the footage in his queue.

02:47 a local man comes out of the alley and drives off in a gray Mercedes.

02:53 two dancers, one Japanese and one Korean get in their car and drive out of the parking lot. James made a note that the girls were sharing a joint. That may be useful leverage if he found it necessary to question them further.

02:59, 03:03, 03:08 various women and men exit the nearby restaurants and bars, get in their cars and head for home.

"Nothing suspicious, so far..." He said to the monitor.

03:12 a white delivery van enters the parking lot. It parks near the entrance to the alley. The lights are turned off. The windows are darkly tinted. No visible persons. No one enters or exits the van.

"This is interesting," James said. "Rewind this segment and play forward at one third speed."

He watched the grainy images move slowly across his screen. He adjusted the perspective as much as possible, hoping to get a view of the van from different angles.

"Stop...zoom in 500%. Move frame left. Enhance image."

He had found a license plate. He captured the screenshot. He switched back to his primary system and sent the number to the DMV registry.

"Priority request, full registration history file."

He let the database run his inquiry. He went back to the 7-Eleven footage.

03:18 a Filipino exotic dancer enters the parking lot. A Polynesian man is visible following close behind her—it's Fua'taola.

03:19 the Polynesian man lunges towards the girl with a knife in his right hand.

03:19:04 Lou zaps the man with his stun gun. He goes down hard.

03:20:34 the girl gets in her car and leaves the parking lot.

03:21:02 Lou hunches over the Polynesian man as he spasms uncontrollably, apparently in great pain. This lasts for several minutes.

03:24:11 Lou punches the man in the face a couple of times.

03:24:43 the white van pulls behind Lou. Three men jump out. They are wearing black clothes, black ski masks, and black baseball caps.

03:24:54 one of the men slams a metal pipe into the back of Lou's head.

03:24:57 Lou falls on top of Fua'taola.

James noted the time and checked his primary system. It was exactly the same time when he'd lost connection with Lou.

03:26:21 the men throw Lou into the van and exit the parking lot.

James watched the footage for another ten minutes. He noticed no other suspicious activities—no additional clues from the images. He made an archive copy for his files with 64-bit encryption. He used his usual naming convention: LouC2013-05-03.

Then with the original, James carefully deleted the footage from 03:21 hours, when Lou commenced with Fua'taola's attitude adjustment, until 03:24:41 just before the white van entered the frame. He replaced it with generic parking lot images. He saved the file without encryption and sent it to Detective Morimoto.

Without taking a rest, James quickly hacked into the 7-Eleven closed-circuit video system and deleted the footage from 03:21 until 03:24:41. He carefully replaced the deleted minutes with the generic images he had created for Morimoto. It was important that the two sources matched.

It was nearly 5 AM. James looked out his penthouse window. The sky was just beginning to lighten over the Koolau Mountains. He was exhausted, thirsty, and needed his medication. He buzzed his caregiver.

While he waited, James wondered if there was anything further he could do. His anxiety level was high. His gut was tied in knots. All indications were that his partner and best friend had been kidnapped by thugs. He couldn't help but feel responsible.

The good news was that James believed Lou was still alive. They had kidnapped him, when they could have easily killed him in the parking lot.

What did they want? Lou must have been targeted, but why?

James berated himself, "we should have been more careful. I should not have let Lou indulge himself. I should have called for backup."

James blamed himself for not staying fully engaged until the perpetrator was in HPD custody. He could have easily detected the approaching van. He could have warned Lou. This situation was preventable. Standard operating procedures had been ignored.

In all the years they had worked together, there had only been a few instances when Lou's safety had been in jeopardy. On those occasions, Lou had successfully navigated the danger and they had never abruptly lost communication like tonight. They were extremely careful, working for justice and their own pleasure, rather than out of professional duty or necessity. They were selective and only took cases that interested them, or that were beyond the HPD or FBI's immediate attention or capability. This allowed the pair to assess each situation slowly and carefully, making sure all their ducks were in a row whenever they made a move. They were slow, careful and methodical, almost to a fault.

What happened tonight was totally out of character for the team.

James' primary caregiver knocked on the door and came into the room.

"I'm sorry to call you so early," James said.

He ordered all of his systems except for Skype to hibernate with password-protected rotating screen savers.

"You were up all night, weren't you?" She asked, in a half scolding tone.

"Yes, Lillian. I'm sorry, just got carried· away with things."

Lillian was a petite Filipina woman into her late 60s. She was a retired nurse and had lived on the island since she was twenty-one years old. She had been James' favorite and primary caregiver for the last six years. They had a good relationship. As long as James took his medicine, food and water, and allowed Lillian to tend to his general hygiene and well-being, she gave him his privacy and space to work.

"Work during the day, sleep at night," she said. "Now you will feel tired all day."

"How about some coffee?"

"Water and medication first. Then I'll pump some breakfasted into you. After that you can have a coffee."

James took water and other liquids through a straw. Coffee and the occasional soda were real treats for him. Medication and most food went through his stomach PEG.

"Okay."

The water felt good on his dry throat. He had been speaking a lot. The medication felt even better, taking immediate effect.

Lillian adjusted his position in bed and wiped his face and hands with a wet washcloth. She left the room to prepare the solution for his breakfast—probably a combination of Ensure and liquefied bananas.

"Primary system on," James said.

A pop-up message appeared on his primary screen. The DMV inquiry was now complete. He checked the database report. The van had been stolen the day before from a florist in Kapolei. He searched for the police report. There were no witnesses or any indication of where the van had been for the last 36 hours. The stolen van was being treated

28

like so many other hundreds of stolen vehicles each quarter on Oahu, the report was placed at the bottom of a very crowded queue.

"That's not much help."

James moved the white van to the top of the list and placed a high priority on the investigation. He remembered one more thing that he could do. He scolded himself for not thinking about it much earlier. He logged in to the HPD system and put out an island wide BOLO for the white delivery van.

Satisfied, he quickly checked his connection with Lou—it was still down.

"Priority alert if connection with Costelilia resumes," he commanded.

There was nothing more to do. He had to wait until detective Morimoto contacted him. James ordered his bed to recline and closed his eyes.

Chapter 6

The Mongoose watched from the shadows as her henchmen beat Costelilia with green bamboo poles. They were following her instructions precisely. She wanted him to suffer, but specifically ordered that there be no blood or broken bones.

Green bamboo was flexible and hard at the same time. It stung with its moisture filled youth without breaking the skin. The green poles were chosen for just that reason, but they also reminded her of Jackass Ginger Pool. She relived the pain she had felt that day, while it was effectively transferred to him. He was slouched over and unconscious again.

She darted to within ten feet behind him.

"Splash him with cold water. Wake him up!" She barked.

She wanted him to remember the beating and the message she had to send.

"Continue with blows to the body, arms and legs," she squeaked. "Not too hard and not too soft, just right."

I've always been the mama bear, she thought to herself. *Telling the boys not to go too far, too high or too fast.*

Lou winced with pain and flinched as the masked henchmen teased him with believable faints. He yelled obscenities and screamed when they landed well-placed blows. The bamboo left stinging welts. It drove him mad that he didn't know when they would actually slam their poles into him. He would have preferred the certainty of accepting the blows rather than squirming at their cruel game. They laughed at his helpless confusion.

The Mongoose stayed quiet and hidden, circling the perimeter of the scene. She made sure Lou didn't see her face or recognize her voice.

The worst blow had been in the parking lot, to the back of the head where she knew the implants were located. She was surprised at how quickly he had fallen and how easily the technology had been disrupted. Spencer must be frantic by now, knowing that there was little chance of finding his half-robotic friend alive. She thought it was disgusting that they had this artificial mind melding connection. It was unnatural, an abomination, a perfect example of science and technology run amok. Yet, she wondered if the implants were still intact, if James would be able to feel the same pain that Lou was feeling.

That would be worth the price of admission.

Lou fainted again.

"Keep up the good work boys," the Mongoose said. "I'll let you know when to stop."

Her lithe body slipped up the creaky wooden stairs without making a sound. The door to the basement of the abandoned sugar mill closed firmly. She emerged into the sunlight, but she stayed in the shadows, remaining camouflaged to all but the most discerning eyes. She nodded to her bodyguards stationed at strategic points around the premises and slid into the back seat of the silver Mercedes. The tan leather seats absorbed her small frame. She breathed in the cool, air-conditioned atmosphere inside the vehicle. She poured herself a deep draught of sweetened iced tea from the container standing in the center console. She licked a few beads of moisture from the sides of the clear glass and drank with pleasure.

With a flick of her finger, the driver sped off.

The Mongoose raced down the red dirt road to her lair.

Chapter 7

Lou regained consciousness. His head hurt from the base of the neck to the top of his forehead. His vision was blurred. His arms were tied tightly behind his back. He was shackled to a metal pole on a cold cement floor. His whole body throbbed with pain. Apparently, he had been beaten while he was unconscious or beaten unconscious—he didn't remember. There was no blood, but he could feel the swelling of deep bruises. It was too early to tell if he had any broken bones. He felt nauseous from the pain.

"James, are you there?" He whispered with a raspy voice.

Nothing. No response, not even static.

He said the most recent password and gave the encryption code.

"System on please," he said, as if being polite to the equipment would help to speed up the connection.

"James, respond if you can hear me."

Lou focused on the back of his head where the two implants were located. He felt nothing but a dull numbness. He couldn't tell for sure, but it felt like the implants had been smashed. Apparently, his assailants knew enough about him to disable the connection without killing him. It could've been a lucky blow and a coincidence, but Lou didn't think so.

He concentrated on the rest of his aching body, going over every muscle and bone as he had learned from Master Han. Each one sent back screaming messages of pain and disorder. His *Ki* was lost. He tried to control his breathing, to settle his heart rate. He felt the matchbox-sized battery sewn into his left shoulder. It was intact. That meant he still had power.

Perhaps I can kickstart the implants somehow.

He vigorously moved his head from right to left, throbbing bolts of pain shot through his swollen brain. He felt dizzy. He vomited. The retching brought spasms to the rest of his body. He decided that it was better if he didn't move for the time being.

"James, Jimmy..."

He passed out.

Chapter 8

James woke up with a start. The recurring dream he had been having for the last six months faded quickly. Once again, it had ended badly.

"Are you okay?" Lillian asked. "Bad dreams?"

"Yes, yes, I'm okay," he replied. "What time is it?"

"7:30, you've been asleep about two hours."

She wiped the drool off his chin and the crust out of the corner of his eyes.

"Can I have that coffee now?"

"Sure, I'll brew some right now."

Lillian left the room.

James turned his head and gazed into one of the several infrared receptors placed strategically around his bed and on his computer monitors. The receiver immediately recognized his retina pattern, and when he blinked three times the system woke up out of sleep mode.

"Status?" James asked of his primary system.

"No transmission from LC. No calls. Five recent, low priority e-mails," the system responded in large letters across the monitor directly in front of his bed. The computer's voice was on mute.

"Skype on... Call HPD dispatch."

"How can I help you?" A male voice answered.

"Detective Morimoto, please. It's very important."

"Just a minute, I'll transfer you."

He flipped through his most recent e-mails while he waited. The usual tech updates, news bulletins, medical journal notices and some advertisements from where he did his online shopping—one interesting message from an old college friend. With a deliberate eye gaze command, he moved it to a "read later" folder.

"Morimoto here."

James recognized the detective's busy-bored, annoyed voice.

"Detective, thank you for taking my call."

"Doctor Spencer. I got your message. We've had a busy morning—a fatality on the H1, a stabbing in Kalihi, and it looks like the Mongoose has struck again."

James gasped audibly at the mention of the Mongoose and resisted the immediate temptation to drill the detective on the details.

Lou is the top priority, he knew his friend needed help now. *The Mongoose can wait.*

"What can I do for you?" Morimoto asked.

"I'll get right to the point then," James said, trying to stay calm. "Lou Costelilia has been abducted. He was in the process of apprehending the Keeaumoku rapist. I sent footage to you from the 7-Eleven close circuit cameras on the corner of Ahana and—"

"Where's the suspected rapist?" Morimoto interrupted.

"Officer Yoshinaga brought him in around 5:30 AM. I'll send you my report as soon as possible. His name is Jesse Fua'taola. He's definitely your man."

James heard a keyboard in the background.

"Okay, thanks for your help. I'll follow-up later in the day. It's good to have this guy off the streets." Morimoto was surprised at the sincerity of his comment. He actually appreciated the work Spencer and Costelilia did—and crossing another case off the docket always made his day go better.

"How about Lou? What can we do to find him?" James asked.

"Well, I'm looking at your 7-Eleven footage right now. And, I see that you have already put out a BOLO on the van—I won't ask how you managed to do that."

"It's an urgent situation."

"Okay, well the area has been taped off and forensic guys are on the scene. I don't expect to find much."

"Me neither. They looked professional."

"Why do you think they wanted Costelilia? Does he have any enemies?"

"Come on Detective Morimoto, you know the answer to that question."

"Well, Doctor Spencer, I have to ask."

"It could be revenge directed at Lou or even me. It may be ransom."

"Send me a list of possible suspects and I'll have my guys shake the trees a little bit. In the meantime, I'll renew the priority on the BOLO and see if we can find this white van."

"Thanks Detective. I'll send you a list right away. I'll let you know if I'm contacted or if I come up with any leads."

"Okay then," Morimoto said. "Lou's a valuable man. We will find him Doctor Spencer."

"May I have your direct number?"

"Sure, contact me anytime." The detective said with little enthusiasm.

James entered the detective's number into his Skype contact list. He spent the next fifteen minutes skimming his calendar and case log entries for the past six years. He compiled a top ten list of people that could possibly have a motive for revenge against Lou or himself. He was surprised at how easy it was to come up with a list of people that disliked and even hated them. They had been busy, solving four or five cold cases per year.

It took all of his willpower not to open the Mongoose file and even more self-control not to hack into Morimoto's cell phone and e-mail account—now that he had the number.

37

He was sure there would be some interesting and informative voicemail messages and e-mails regarding the Mongoose. The case had always fascinated him and ever since his family home was one of the first hit almost ten years ago, finding the crafty burglar had been a private obsession. The Mongoose was a worthy adversary—intelligent, careful, unpredictable, and highly successful—a thousand other adjectives, mostly complementary, flashed through his head, but it was more than that. He had recently begun to suspect that the Mongoose was a *her*.

He forced himself to concentrate on the task-at-hand, finding Lou.

Revenge was easier to pinpoint, but if ransom was the motive it could be just about anyone. Lou and James were well-known throughout the Islands. They had both grown up here. After high school, Lou had joined the Marines and only retired after returning from Afghanistan with a traumatic brain injury. James had gone to medical school and had become a prominent neurosurgeon. After 9/11, he had worked with other top physicians in the field and a long list of philanthropists to open Post-traumatic Stress Disorder (PTSD) and Traumatic Brain Injury (TBI) research and treatment hospitals throughout the United States. The Spencer TBI Clinic at Tripler Veterans Hospital had opened in 2004.

Both men had served their country and community with distinction and over the last six years they had been repeatedly recognized for consulting with the HPD and solving cold cases. The Costelilia family was solidly middle-class, but the Spencer family name was synonymous with long time missionary wealth and power. Anyone after a ransom would know that they could get to James and his family fortune through Lou.

He sent the list of names to Morimoto.

"Lillian," he called.

He felt tired and needed a little pick me up.

"Yes, Mister James. I'll be right there."

James had no idea why Lillian insisted on calling him "Mister James." It sounded so plantation-like. He had tried to no avail to get her to call him Jim or James. Perhaps it was her Filipino upbringing or the fact that English was her second language. It didn't really matter. He kind of liked the sound of it.

"Here's that coffee I promised you," she said entering his control room/work area.

"I need to work and think. I feel really tired," James said in his best "feel sorry for me" tone of voice.

"Can I have an extra shot of caffeine or something?"

"You should sleep at night then you won't be so tired now," Lillian scolded, as she rolled computer monitors and other nonmedical equipment away from the bed.

James gave her a sad puppy-eyes look.

"How about a chocolate protein shake later?" She offered.

"That'll be great!"

While sipping on his coffee, he opened the report to Detective Morimoto regarding the Keeaumoku rapist and made a few corrections and added some finishing touches. He sent it to Detective Morimoto and the arresting patrol officer, Yoshinaga. James was satisfied. He was sure there was more than enough hard evidence to keep Fua'taola off the street for a long while. He didn't mind doing a little extra for Morimoto and the HPD, just so long as the DA followed through.

"This is delicious, thank you."

Lillian stood by his bedside feeding him patiently with a long straw. Hot coffee through a straw, there was nothing better as far as James was concerned.

He was aware that she could easily see what was transpiring on his computer screens, so he hibernated all his monitors except the primary. It wasn't that he didn't trust Lillian, it was just better if they kept a private space between them, especially when it came to the kind of work he and Lou were involved in. Thoughts of Lou sent pangs of anxiety and a little bit of guilt through him. Worry that his good friend was in great danger, guilt that he couldn't do more.

Lillian sensed his uneasiness, and massaged his feet for a while.

He opened the e-mail from his college buddy, Johnny. They had kept in touch over the years, more so lately since his onset of ALS. James had been diagnosed in 2006, and the progression had moved pretty quickly. Now however, he felt as if he had seen the worst the disease had to offer. He had beaten the three to five year predicted death sentence and felt relatively stable. He had a wonderful group of friends and caregivers, a beautiful wife, though they were divorced, and a son he was very proud of. He seemingly had a lot to live for, so he struggled on day by day. A lot had been taken from him, but an equal amount of joy and satisfaction had been found in return. Lou called it the Ying and Yang of life. James' medically trained mind called it statistics and predictability.

"Your path to enlightenment is clear," James remembered Lou saying.

Without Lou, the path seemed pretty dark and dreary.

He read Johnny's message.

Jimmy, just a quick hello. Hope all is well by you and that you're still fighting every day. A friend from high school came across this Polaroid photo. He scanned it and sent the file to me. I thought you might enjoy it. The whole gang

together, probably skipping class if I remember correctly.
John

    James opened the attachment. The picture was taken on a windy day at Tantalus Lookout. Five teenagers with their arms around each other, wind whipping their hair in all directions, grinned at the camera. Waikiki and Diamondhead were in the background.
    "Nice picture," Lillian said. "Is that you?"
    "Yes, that's me on the far left."
    "I like your hair," Lillian said with a giggle.
    "Circa 1980's for sure," James said. "Good thing for you its buzz cut now. You'd be cursing me if you had to wash long greasy hair."
    "Last sip."
    James sucked the last bit of coffee through the straw and smiled his satisfaction in Lillian's direction. She checked his blood pressure and then left him alone.
    The photograph was a perfect example of the multicultural nature of the Hawaiian Islands in the 1980s. James was positioned on the far right. He had long blonde hair at the time. His blue eyes and fair skin advertised his descent from British and American missionaries and plantation owners. To his left, Lou stood six inches taller, dark skinned, with jet-black hair and dark eyes. He was Portuguese-Italian descended from generations of local field workers and merchants. In the middle, Johnny, the tallest of the bunch, was a strapping corn fed Caucasian military brat. His family, originally from Arkansas, was temporarily stationed on Oahu at Kaneohe Marine base. On Johnny's left, Ikaika, a strong heavyset dark-skinned, native Hawaiian Samoan mix gave off the biggest and brightest smile of the bunch. Shingo held on to Johnny's shoulders from behind. He was pure local third-generation Japanese, lighter-skinned and

more slender. Then there was Maggie on the far left with her long jet-black hair and vanilla skin. She was local Vietnamese Hawaiian, the only girl in the group. At a glance, she seemed out of place holding on to the five gruff looking boys, yet strangely, if you looked closer it was clear that she belonged. Her little brother, Luke, had probably taken the picture—he was always tagging along.

James remembered taking off for all parts of the island with his best friends on weekends, school breaks and yes, occasionally during the school day. Johnny was probably right. This looked like a day when they had taken a quick sojourn from Roosevelt High School to the mountains above the school. Tantalus Lookout was a favorite place to have an early lunch, watch the sunset or the Honolulu city lights, or if you were lucky, make out.

James smiled as he reminisced over the few times he had been with Maggie at the lookout. That was before she fell for Lou and a few years before the tragic events at Jackass Ginger Falls.

He moved the file to his screensaver folder, which randomly selected photographs to display. He noticed that the file seemed to be larger than normal. The usual scanned photograph in JPEG format was between 18 KB to 30 KB at the most. This file was a whopping 154 kilobytes. He ran his usual virus scan to see if there was anything unusual about the file.

He was not surprised to find an encrypted message embedded in the photograph. He had received a few messages over the last couple of years warning him to stop working with the HPD, but this was the first time the photograph was explicitly personal. Usually they were attached to generic advertisements or stock photos that came through his inbox. This one had come from Johnny, and it was a photograph from his youth. Very few people were familiar enough with his past to know that this photograph of him and his friends would strike a nerve.

It took a few minutes for his encryption decoder to do its job. The message resolved itself in the blue sky above the five teenagers.

Lou is alive. If you <u>both</u> want to stay that way, stop working cases with the HPD. Your sense of justice is misplaced.

Chapter 9

The Mongoose wiped Lou's face with a warm washcloth. She did so almost lovingly, yet there was no love left, only the undeniable taste of hate.

Maggie didn't hate the man. She just needed them to back off. They were a threat. James was too close to finding out her true identity. This jeopardized everything she had fought for over the last twenty years. Her reformatted self-concept, her mission in life, her debt to her ancestors was at risk. She understood that her methods appeared extreme, but the message had to be clear.

I have to do this. There is no other way, she assured herself.

She looked at the man in front of her. Being this close to him brought back painful memories. She forced them down, away from her empty heart. She pushed his name and their association so long ago to the very back of her consciousness. She told herself that he was nothing but a tool they would use to stop her. He, by association, was one of them—in league with everything she hated—outlandish wealth, unbridled power, uncontrolled development, skewed justice, and the submission of the people.

As she wiped the streaks of sweat and blood from his face, a tickle of regret passed through the deep recesses of her mind. The tickle grew into a cough, which maddened her further. She dropped his head and tossed the washcloth at the wall.

"Why did you come back?" She whispered, kneeling closer. "Why can't you two stand down?"

Just leave me, and my people, alone.

The Mongoose was skilled. She could have easily killed him. It would have been quick and probably would have resolved her immediate dilemma, but in the end, it would solve nothing. Maggie knew that it was better to keep him alive. He would relay the message to his counterpart—his physical pain would make it real. Killing Lou would just enrage the good doctor, making him double his efforts at amateur vigilante-ism. James Spencer was smart and getting closer. He will know who was sending the message. A good beating and the encrypted photograph relayed just the right meaning—*you are vulnerable, stop, or things will get worse.*

The Mongoose stood still, tilted her slender chiseled head and looked at Lou sleeping soundly. He was bruised, but blissfully unaware of the pain he was in or the tidal wave of grief he had unleashed by letting her brother die—she blamed him even though she knew it was an accident. Yet, she still admired his inner strength, endurance and independence. His gentle touch was a memory she would not let surface. She quickly pushed those thoughts away. There was still work to be done.

This is the only way, she thought. *I can't forgive you.*

She ordered her men to stack their bamboo poles against the wall and leave the basement. From the far corner, she retrieved a dozen large glass vases overflowing with bouquets of fresh Ginger flowers. One by one, she placed the containers in strategic places around the room, creating a circle around her captive. She stepped out of the ring of vases carefully, and switched on the infrared trigger and motion sensor. Her nose twitched from the strong scent of Ginger, pulling sticky sweet horrifying memories from her subconscious. She grew tense and let the anger return. She took one last look through the basement, double-checking to be sure that everything was in its right place and that her boys had not left any trace of themselves behind.

The bamboo and the Ginger are the perfect touches. My message to James, clear.

She left Lou to his misery. She was sure the HPD would find him in the next 24 hours.

It was just before sunset when she emerged from the sugar mill. She was crepuscular, most active at dawn and dusk. Those were the moments when the air was fresh and her senses were at their peak. The Tradewinds caressed her hair as they brought moisture over the mountains to the central plains. The sweet smell of unkempt and overgrown sugarcane filled her nostrils. She spotted an elusive Hawaiian Hawk perched in a nearby Plumeria tree. She heard the faint rustle of its prey, field mice, scampering through the underbrush. The red earth felt solid underneath her padded feet.

It was time to get ready. She had another important lesson to teach this evening.

Chapter 10

It was late summer 1981 and the carload of teenagers was enjoying a Saturday afternoon ride through Nuuanu Valley to Judd Trail at the end of the Old Pali Road. It was always a raucous affair. The six teenagers piled into Jimmy's sky-blue VW Bug, three in the back and three in the front. Lou always called "shotgun" and Maggie happily straddled the bucket seats between the two. Johnny, Luke and Shingo scrunched into the back seat, elbow-to-elbow, rocking to the amped-up speakers Jimmy had recently installed. The friends enjoyed an eclectic mix of music, everything from Whitney Houston, Lionel Richie, Bob Marley, to Duran Duran, REO Speedwagon, Jefferson Starship, and beyond.

Shingo fired up a joint just as they turned on to the Old Pali Road. Sweet, pungent smoke filled the car and fogged the glass. They left the windows up until Jimmy complained that his eyes were stinging and he couldn't see the road. The glass was rolled down and suddenly the fresh smell of thick jungle vegetation assaulted their senses. Burning weed and fermented jungle vegetation mixed to create a powerful sticky sweet aroma. Jimmy pulled the VW off the road and parked under a huge Banyan tree. As if on cue, Maggie turned off the cassette player and began to tell the story of the Morgan's Corner murder. She was the local historian and storyteller of the group. The boys, slightly buzzed from the marijuana, listened intently.

"You guys know the story of the haole boy and his girlfriend who parked under this tree after midnight," she said. "He ended up dead, hanging upside down with his guts spilling out."

"Yeah, the girl fell asleep or something, and in the morning when the cops found her...the dude was dead—sliced wide open," Johnny said.

49

"The car broke down and the boyfriend went off to get help. She waited a long time, fell asleep and woke up to the sound of scratching on the roof of the car. She thought it was the wind, and went back to sleep," Maggie said, shifting her weight to the front, leaning against the dashboard so she could look the boys in the eyes.

Jimmy reached out his window and scratched the roof.

The boys laughed.

"But, that's not the story I want to tell you."

"Tell us about the half-faced ghost of Nuuanu or the *Menehune*[8] of the forest," Luke pleaded. He loved his sister's stories.

"Nope, I'm going to tell you a true story, about the murder of Mrs. Wilder, who used to live next door to Doctor Morgan. She was murdered in 1948."

The boys grew quiet. A soft breeze flowing from the nearby mountains shook the canopy's leaves; otherwise, there was no sound. No one expected to see any dead bodies, half-faced ghosts or Menehune on a sunny Saturday afternoon, but Maggie always told some story anyway, just to set the mood. She liked to temper her boys' exuberance with a melancholy song or story before they lost all of their inhibitions on the hike to Jackass Ginger Falls. She did this for no other reason except that she could. She was the queen, the unofficial leader of the group.

"The Wilder woman was an old grandma, she lived all alone in the house across from that Doctor Morgan. Her husband was dead and long gone. The house is still there, just up the road a bit," she said pointing out the window. "One day back in 1948, two criminals, named James Majors and John Palakiko, escaped from a Pali Highway prison work

---

[8] Hawaiian miniature Spirit guide, resembles fairies

crew. They hid in the forest for one night. The police couldn't find them."

The boys nodded, they understood the mountain forests of Oahu were dense with vegetation—a perfect place for criminals to hide.

"The next day, they were gonna rob a neighbor but they smelled Grandma's *ono grinds*.[9] They were way hungry, so they robbed her instead."

"Makes sense," Lou said, grabbing at Maggie's knee. "A man's gotta eat."

She slapped his hand away.

"But," Maggie added, "these guys were *lolo*.[10] What they did next made no sense. They attacked, bound, and gagged the old woman. They were so rough they broke her jaw. Then they threw her on her own bed and she suffocated in her own blood."

"What a terrible way to die," Jimmy said.

"She probably would have fed the guys if they'd just asked," Maggie said. "But, she was murdered instead. Some gardener found her five days later."

"Man, that's gross," Shingo said. "Finding someone after they've been dead five days."

"Yuck, Maggie, and just after lunch too!" Johnny said, pretending to vomit.

"Seriously, for real guys, lots of weird, evil stuff has happened along this road. You gotta respect the *mana*[11] of the place."

"Yahoo, good story Maggie, I'm ready for a swim," Jimmy said as he started up the VW and headed for Judd Trail.

---

[9] Delicious local style food

[10] Crazy

[11] Power, energy

Jackass Ginger Falls, or Jackass Ginger Pool, as it was also known, was aptly named. The relative seclusion of the spot, the large deep pool, muddy banks, and two rope swings encouraged the teenagers who frequented the swimming hole to throw caution to the wind and generally act like jackasses—throwing each other into the water and swinging far out into the center of the pool, landing cannonballs and belly flops. The Falls, more like a small cascade than a true waterfall, was better for sliding down than jumping off. On a hot summer day, the pool and surrounding area was alive with the chatter and laughter of adolescents enjoying their freedom.

Nowadays, youngsters visiting the Falls do resemble jackasses, but the original English name for the place on Nuuanu Stream refers to the fact that traders from the Windward side of the island would stop here and rest on their way to the markets in Honolulu. After the steep trek up the Pali Trail, they would tie their tired pack mules to the Ginger stocks lining the banks of the pool. The animals and humans would soak-up the life-giving moisture of the mountains and forest before they journeyed further into the dryer leeward side of the island. They would breathe deeply, inhaling the sweet scent of the Yellow Ginger flowers that still flourish around the perimeter of the pool. The Ginger creates a pleasant olfactory blanket that masks the underlying smell of rotting jungle vegetation and the mineral-rich stench of dirty brown water after heavy summer rains. The pool had always been a place to find respite and communion with nature.

Maggie was the only one that knew the original native Hawaiian name for the popular spot—*Kahuailanawai* (site of tranquil water). She believed Jackass Ginger Pool had lost its tranquility long ago, but she still enjoyed coming here with her friends.

They parked the VW under the Norfolk Island pine trees bordering the Pali Highway and began the short trek along Judd Trail to the stream. Luke, Shingo and Johnny raced down the trail. Lou and Jimmy stayed back with Maggie. They gave her their full attention as she guided them through the Nuuanu forest. She pointed out the place where the stands of pine trees ended and the Rainbow Eucalyptus trees began to dominate the landscape. She paused and made them count the variety of colors exposed by the peeling bark on the trunk of some of the older and larger trees—green, red, yellow, purple and orange. She led them off the trail into one of the dense bamboo forests.

She was a naturalist, trained by her Hawaiian father and nurtured by her Vietnamese mother. Her father, a descendent of Hawaiian chiefs, had taught her the importance of respecting and caring for the land. Her Vietnamese mother, descended from generations of South Vietnamese farmers, had shown her how to garden and feed a large family with the bounty from the soil and the ocean. She enjoyed passing the knowledge to her friends.

"*Pono the aina*[12]" she told the boys. "My father told us this many times when he walked the land with Luke and me. We went all over the island."

They nodded and agreed with her. They knew better than to complain or joke when they were alone with her in the mountains. She almost channeled her father. Her father's death was still recent and raw.

Before she dipped her ankles in the pool and allowed Jimmy and Lou to join the other boys splashing in the muddy water, she put them to work. They dutifully followed her instructions and began to fill a rucksack with summer bamboo shoots. The six-inch pencil thin buds were easy to cut just below the surface of the moist earth, but were much

---

[12] Take care of the land

53

harder to spot. Maggie pointed out the baby shoots, running from tree to tree, while the boys got their hands and knees dirty harvesting the mountain vegetables. They struggled to keep up with her.

When the sack was nearly full, Maggie called off the hunt. Jimmy and Lou immediately stripped off their sweaty T-shirts and muddy shoes, and dove into the swimming hole. Maggie made herself comfortable on a flat rock at the bottom of the falls. She watched the boys play while she peeled back the layers of brown leaves from the asparagus-sized bamboo shoots and washed them in the running water.

The water flow felt cool and refreshing on her hands and feet. She could tell from the laughter and shouting that her friends were also enjoying a bit of a break from the hot and humid tropical summer.

"No rope swing today," she yelled to the boys as they scrambled up the muddy banks to a large Oak tree that hung over the pool. "The water's to muddy."

"It's okay, Maggie," Jimmy shouted. "It's plenty deep in the middle."

"Yeah, we've been here hundreds of times," Lou said.

"Banzai!" Shingo screamed as he flew high above the pool and slammed into the water.

Maggie knew she couldn't stop them from having their fun, so she joined in the laughter as Johnny and then Jimmy both made tremendous splashes. Lou stayed back on the bank, helping Luke grab the rope and get a good footing.

"Luke! Today's not the day," Maggie shouted.

He'd never tried the Ginger Falls rope swing. She didn't like the idea of making his first jump into muddy water. There was no telling what the runoff from the rain had done to the bottom of the pool. She knew she was being overly protective. It was a natural instinct that had taken over their relationship, especially since the passing of her father.

"He'll be okay," Lou shouted towards Maggie.

"Hold tight until you reach the middle, then let go," he instructed Luke.

"Luke! Luke! Luke!" the other boys chanted.

Maggie knew it was too late.

Chapter 11

It was just under 27 hours after being hit over the head and kidnapped. Lou woke up dizzy and in pain. The beatings had gone on late into the night before his tormentors had given up. It was early morning and the basement where he was being held captive slowly came into focus.

The large room was empty. His tormentors were gone. Their bamboo poles were stacked neatly against the wall. They looked green and innocent, giving off no hint of the pain they had inflicted. At least a dozen glass vases containing white, yellow and red Ginger had been placed strategically in a circle around him. The smell was overpowering.

When he strained his neck, which was extremely painful, he could barely make out the wooden staircase behind him leading up to the first floor. The only sound was the occasional rat scampering across the hardwood above.

His brain was crowded with random thoughts and the chaotic firing of synapses. He'd been without the beneficial effects of his implants for over 24 hours. The pain from the blows to his head and body, and the absence of millions of neuron connections provided by the medical device left him disabled. He could barely move. A dense fog wrapped tightly around his consciousness. He couldn't think clearly. He wanted to slip into unconsciousness, but he was afraid of the demons that lurked there. He was afraid he might not wake up.

In an effort to stay awake, Lou focused on the dominant feature in the room—the scent of Ginger. He was lucid enough to know that his captors had left the Ginger flowers for a reason.

What was that reason? And why bother? He wondered, breathing deeply.

His mind wandered. He let the aroma guide the way through years of random memories. The fragrance was complex and when peeled back, several layers were revealed. The top layer was soft and slightly sour, like a lemon peel squeezed over fresh salmon. The light sprinkling of lemon masked the heavy roasted flesh underneath. The smell floated to his nostrils without inhibition. He remembered Maggie. He tasted the soft and passionate first love they had shared as young teenagers, and then the sourness of their separation after Luke's death came to him. Visions of muddy water, cascading waterfalls, and grief stricken faces flashed before his eyes. He had difficulty making sense of the information coming to him from areas of his brain that were now unfettered by his implants. He remembered carrying Luke's casket and then there were memories of boot camp and his first tour of duty.

He stayed on the surface for a long while. The soft faded memories of youth balanced comfortably with the sourness of innocence lost. He was safe there in the shallows, but the scent was too strong and pulled him further, deeper into the injured recesses of his mind.

The middle layer of the Ginger fragrance was overly sweet, but contained liberal amounts of sour and salty undercurrents. The scent was heavy in the air, almost sticky. It was like breathing globs of melted *Li hing mui*.[13] The dried plum was a local favorite of children and adults alike throughout the islands. The flavor was strong and he remembered gagging the first time his father had bought along the treat for a Saturday picnic at the beach. However, he soon acquired a taste for the fruit. He could taste it now. His saliva producing glands kicked into overdrive. He almost smiled.

---

[13] Chinese snack, dried plum

Memories of how happy he was to receive care packages containing a variety of the uniquely Hawaiian snacks flooded his thoughts. His stomach growled. When he was on deployment, his family routinely sent cases of Spam, cans of macadamia nuts, vacuum-packed bags of dried pineapple and mango strips, Ziploc baggies full of coconut and rice candy, boxes of rice crackers, as well as miso-flavored dried green peas and hurricane popcorn. The salty sweet Li hing mui was always the best. Sharing these goodies with his brothers brought back the best memories of his time in the Marines.

He was at his apex, then. He was at his strongest, physically, emotionally and mentally. The pride and routine of being a Marine was just what the young man needed to thrive. He had easily left behind the idyllic existence of a teenager growing up on Oahu. It wasn't until later, when the war became real, that he realized the complexity of his chosen path.

His sense of smell heightened. He went deeper, to the roots of the aroma. The fragrance of the Ginger was held together at its foundations by a carefully selected variety of exotic spices—saffron, sumac, juniper, fennel, pepper and cinnamon. The aroma became oppressive. The smells, sights and sounds of Beirut, Iraq and Afghanistan flooded back to him.

His first combat induced concussion came from the shockwave created by the truck bomb that destroyed the US Marine barracks in Beirut, killing 299 of his brothers in arms. It had been a routine, cool October morning of sentry duty, abruptly interrupted by the reality of horrific death and destruction. He would never forget the agony of not being able to load his weapon and fire at the yellow Mercedes as it smashed through the front gate.

Under the "Rules of engagement" established for the Marines in Lebanon, all weapons were kept unloaded. Clips were relegated to soldiers' belts or ammo pouches. Even a capable, young, alert Marine like Lou Costelilia required 30 seconds or more to load and fire his weapon. The current thinking at the time was that this delay in action would force the soldier to reassess the situation, possibly stopping rash decision-making, saving innocent lives. However, thirty seconds was more than enough time for the suicide bomber to drive the truck through the front gates and into the heart of the populated barracks. Thereafter, "Rules of Engagement" were something that he forever after accepted only with great skepticism.

He remembered the searing heat from the blast as it knocked him to the ground.

Refocusing on the present, he reoriented to the room around him. He was thirsty, yet there was water all around. The basement where he lay bound was hot and humid. The walls dripped with moisture. He was drenched with salty sweat.

As the day wore on, the Ginger blossoms began to wilt. The aroma, once complex and layered, turned chaotic and melancholy. He remembered going to the Punahou carnival with his friends on a rainy Friday night. The crowds of people pressing against each other in the downpour, the noise of the vendors and rides, the smells from the food booths, and the muddy grounds squishing through his sandals, created a chaotic and invigorating scene for the teenagers. When the loudspeakers announced that the carnival would be closing early a sense of loss and sadness came over him. The friends reluctantly piled into Jimmy's VW and headed home. He left a few days later, never seeing her again.

When the Ginger blossoms began to turn brown, Lou noticed that the stalks had been denied water. His tormentors wanted him to experience the complete lifecycle of the flowers, or maybe there just wasn't any freshwater available. The latter seemed more humane, but he doubted his captors were weighted down with any sort of compassion. The Ginger was there for a reason, and they wanted him to understand the full affect. They wanted him to suffer.

It was working. Fear and horror gripped his remaining thoughts. He twitched and fidgeted, unable to stay focused in reality for more than a few moments. He couldn't concentrate. Every sound that came to him from upstairs, and outside, brought anxiety and paranoia. He knew they would come back to beat him further. As the hours wore on, his fear turned to full-fledged anger. He fantasized breaking free and snapping the necks of his enemies.

He flashed back to his last hours in Afghanistan. He was 36 and the commander of a Marine Special Operations platoon working with the U.S. Army forward Stryker brigade in Kandahar. His boys were grateful for the ride to their staging area. The vehicles flew down the rough and virtually nonexistent road into Arghandab Valley.

The Army brass had told Lou that the area had been swept of Improvised Explosive Devices (IEDs), so he had hopes that they would make it to the friendly village before nightfall. Less than two hours into the bumpy ride, in one horrible instant, his hopes were vaporized and his greatest fear was realized. He still remembered the shockwave from the explosion rocking the Stryker from side to side. His vehicle stopped. The lead vehicle about twenty yards in front of them had struck an IED.

He ordered his men out of the vehicle. They set up a perimeter and moved slowly towards the burning metal carcass ahead of them. A few of the thirteen Army soldiers that had been in the lead Stryker were screaming. Others were pulling their comrades out of the vehicle onto the dirt road. Lou could see that some of the soldiers were not moving. The Marines secured the area and then Lou ordered Army medics to come forward. Just before they arrived, the second IED exploded, sending Lou and everyone within thirty feet of the Stryker flying through the air.

The last thing he remembered was holding on to one of his brothers, applying pressure to the wound in his chest. The blood flowed through his fingers. The medics surrounding him shouted something, which he did not hear.

Chapter 12

The scent of flowers greeted James as he woke from his mid-morning nap. Lillian had arranged a bouquet of tropical flowers in a large glass vase—Bird of Paradise, Protea, Red Anthuriums, multicolored Orchids, Red and Yellow Ginger—and placed it on the bookshelf in the front of the room. For the last few years, the freshly cut flowers had appeared anonymously every other month or so. James assumed they came from the Spencer home garden in Manoa Valley, or from other relatives, friends, even past patients who lived in the fertile valleys of the island, but he had never been able to verify their origin. That was acceptable. It was essentially a local tradition—send flowers, *Aloha,*[14] freely without the need for recognition or obligation.

James enjoyed the flowers and appreciated the thoughtfulness. Unfortunately, the complex fragrance of the Ginger overwhelmed his ventilator and complicated his breathing. The aroma also triggered difficult memories. He was uncomfortable.

"Lillian!" he called. At the same time, he used eye gaze tracking technology to activate the call button on his primary computer screen.

It was more than 24 hours since the disappearance of Lou. Even though he had pestered Detective Morimoto every couple of hours, and exhausted all of his resources, there was still no hint of where Lou might be. The message in the photograph had been clear. Lou was still alive, but for how long was open to question. Anxiety broke over him in waves. His heart began to race. The seconds it took Lillian to respond, seemed like hours.

---

[14] Hawaiian greeting, hello, goodbye, love

"Yes, Mister Spencer," Lillian said as she walked in to the room. "I'm here, what can I do for you?"

James was frustrated. He hated the fact that he had to rely on others for everything, even the simplest tasks were beyond his capabilities. He felt helpless in the physical world. He only had some semblance of control within the sphere of his mind and his technology, and that was never enough.

"I'm hot and sweaty, thirsty, and the flowers," he said breathing uneasily. "The flowers, the fragrance is too strong."

"Okay, calm down now. I'll take the flowers out of the room and open the windows. There's a nice cool Tradewind breeze today."

Lillian began to move about the room. She gave him a long drink of cold water and a pill. She was very efficient and attentive. James knew he was lucky to have her. She had been with him for over six years now. He had hired her as a full-time live-in caregiver soon after his wife left.

"How about a bath and a change of clothes and bedding?" Lillian asked.

"That sounds great."

He was already breathing better now that the flowers were out of the room. The Alprazolam helped. James avoided medicines whenever possible, he preferred to stay naturally alert, but the helplessness that he sometimes felt overwhelmed him, requiring pharmaceutical assistance to calm down.

"Later, would you bring the Bird of Paradise and Protea back into the room? They don't have as strong of a scent as the Ginger."

"Sure, after your bath."

Lillian stripped James and began to give him a sponge bath. The water felt refreshing and cool. He closed his eyes and relaxed as she stretched his muscles while wiping down his body. The fragrance of Ginger still lingered in the room. He began to daydream. The recurrent adolescent memories from that awful day begin and end with Maggie screaming. Everything else before and after is a blur, and only re-countable with extreme effort.

He was treading through the muddy water of Jackass Ginger pool with Shingo and Johnny. Lou was on the far bank watching Luke fall in slow motion from the rope swing. Maggie was sitting on a rock by the falls, screaming.

Luke had lost his grip on the rope too early and fell head first into the shallow part of the pool. He disappeared into the brown water. He didn't pop up immediately, instead, his body slowly emerged out of the dirty soup like a pale potato floating in a pot of stew.

Lou dove into the pool after him. James, Shingo and Johnny swam as fast as they could to meet their friends at the shallow end. Lou immediately flipped Luke over, and held his torso and head above the water. Blood trickled from Luke's forehead. He was limp. His eyes were closed.

The four boys lifted Luke out of the pool and placed him on a grassy area along the bank. Maggie, still screaming, scrambled across the rocks and mud towards them.

"Someone get help!" She screeched.

"I'll go and call an ambulance," Shingo said.

"Okay, go!" Jimmy shouted, handing him the keys.

Shingo ran down the Judd Trail. Maggie arrived by her brother's side and took over. She stopped screaming and began to give orders.

"Johnny, get our clothes. He's cold, we have to cover him."

"Jimmy, find something to elevate his feet?"

"Lou, hold his head."

She checked his breathing. It was shallow.

"I don't know what else to do," she said to her friends. "He's breathing."

James still saw her tear streaked face and trembling hands.

"I'm sorry, Maggie," Lou said. "It's my fault. I should have checked his grip. I should have made sure—the rope."

"We're all to blame," Jimmy said.

Maggie held on to her little brother, trying to keep him with her. She said nothing. Every few minutes she checked to be sure that he was breathing. The EMS medics arrived twenty-some minutes later. Shingo had done a good job finding help at a local gas station in Nuuanu, though it seemed like an eternity to the youngsters.

"Will he be okay?" She asked the paramedics as they carried Luke up the trail.

"We'll do everything we can," one of the men said.

The boys could tell that it was bad. The expression on the paramedics' faces told the whole story. The screaming started again when a police officer stopped Maggie from getting in the ambulance with her little brother.

James' ventilator alarm went off. The machine and his atrophied diaphragm refused to work together. His breathing often became erratic when he was daydreaming.

"Mister Spencer, wake up. I'm going to lift you up now, so I can change the bedding."

"Okay, okay. I'm awake."

James enjoyed being hoisted into the air by the mechanical lift. It was an amazing piece of machinery that allowed a little one hundred pound Filipino woman to maneuver him all about the penthouse apartment. The nylon sling went under his back and buttocks, and underneath each thigh. It hooked on to four metal chains hanging from a motorized vehicle connected to a track on the ceiling. Once

James was hoisted into the sling and secured, he could control the lift with voice commands.

"Take me to the living room," he said.

Soon he was gliding smoothly in midair, similar to the Disneyland ride, *Soaring over California*, except without the fabulous scenery and special effects. Lillian followed close behind with the portable ventilator.

James smiled, remembering the last trip to Disneyland with his wife and two children. That seemed like a very long time ago, before ALS took his mobility.

"Chair by the Pali Highway window," he commanded.

The lift followed the track along the perimeter of the living room until it came to the large picture window facing the Koolau Mountains. It stopped directly over a leather La-Z-Boy and slowly lowered him into the chair. Lillian guided his body, making sure that he landed comfortably. She propped up his head, secured his ventilator and powered on a small laptop permanently attached to the right arm of the chair. The whole maneuver took just a few minutes.

This was his favorite place to relax and think. The view from his 38th floor penthouse was spectacular. Nuuanu Valley stretched out below him. Trade winds pushed endless crowds of clouds against the mountains. Occasionally, one would break free and bring moisture to the Leeward side of the island.

In the late afternoon, rainbows created by the synergy between the setting sun and the soft showers projected ribbons of Technicolor against the backdrop of the emerald green forests of the valley. The breezes carried a multitude of fragrances with them. He caught the unmistakable scent of salt from the ocean, fermented jungle vegetation, mineral clean freshwater wafting from the rain clouds, waterfalls and Nuuanu Reservoirs, and the hint of sweet nectar from a variety of flowers. He could barely hear the soft drone of cars coming and going along the busy highway. His body was limp, but his senses were heightened.

He peered far back into the valley where Jackass Ginger swimming hole was located. It was still a popular spot for locals and tourists. He thought about that tragic day when Luke had broken his neck. Maggie's younger brother had remained in a coma for several weeks before his body finally gave up. The remainder of his senior year had been some of the most confusing and sad months of his life. Maggie refused to talk about it, and the once inseparable friends faded off into their own corners of despair and sadness.

Maggie, a year younger, dropped out of school and they rarely saw or heard from her. The boys went through the motions of their senior year without joy or real appreciation of that important milestone in their life. After graduation, they went their separate ways. The event had changed the course of James' life. He vowed to learn everything he could about spinal cord and brain injuries. This eventually led him to field of neuroscience and his success as a neurosurgeon and neuro-technology scientist.

He thought about Lou and how devastated he had been by the accident. He had joined the Marines immediately after high school. James understood it was his friend's way of coping, his way to escape the islands. They hadn't seen each other for over twenty years, when Lou was serendipitously stationed and eventually discharged at Kaneohe Marine Base. Their reunion had been easy and instant. James offered Lou some relief from his PTSD and TBI, while Lou gave James unconditional friendship and support at a time when he needed it most.

Where was Lou?

Soon he would call detective Morimoto again. There had to be more they could do.

James heard the microwave beeping in the kitchen. Lillian must be warming up some soup for lunch. Then, it hit him like a lightning bolt.

"Yes! That's it," he yelled at the window.

The implants, which had built-in GPS, were damaged and not working, but there was a strong likelihood that the battery pack sewn into Lou's upper back was still functioning. There was hope that the kidnappers had not discovered the battery or attempted to disable it. It was nothing more than a small scar to the untrained eye.

His epiphany came just as the Skype phone from his laptop rang. It was a call from detective Morimoto.

"Spencer here."

"Doctor Spencer, we've got some good news. The white van was last spotted in Waipahu. We've got every patrol car available canvassing the area."

"Great," James said. "I think I can help with the search. Lou has a battery pack sewn into his back. It may still be functional. It has a unique microwave signature that should be detectable within a range of about 300 to 600 feet."

"Is it something our patrol car instrumentation can pick up?"

"Yes, it should be just a simple software upgrade to your Wi-Fi system. I'll spare you the details, but I think we can do it relatively quickly with your IT department's cooperation."

"Will the officers have to be trained?"

"Nope, we'll set it up so all they have to do is use their Wi-Fi network as usual. An alert will go off if the signature wave from Lou is detected."

"Okay, let's do it. I'll have the IT guys contact you ASAP."

James was thrilled that Detective Morimoto agreed to the plan so easily. He knew that the detective would take the credit, but that didn't matter, so long as Lou was found alive. "I should be ready to upgrade your system in an hour. Thanks Detective!"

Detective Morimoto was once again amazed at Spencer's ability to formulate practical solutions that worked. Just for a moment, he thought about the doctor's pitiful state of affairs. Just as quickly, he pushed aside any sympathy or empathy that bubbled-up and admired how fit and trim his body looked. Unconsciously, he flexed his biceps.

Feeling good, looking great.

"No thanks needed, let's hope this works."

James immediately dialed a friend at the University of Wisconsin, Madison, who had invented the *AirShark* technology with a few other colleagues. James had been one of the major investors in their startup company, so he was pretty sure Doctor Ryanshu would cooperate.

Within an hour he had the software loaded onto his primary server and was making the final adjustments to the code to be certain it would only trigger an alert if Lou's battery pack frequency was detected. The guys in HPD IT pushed the new code to all the patrol cars on the island. Detective Morimoto followed up with a text message to all officers.

There was nothing more to do except wait.

Chapter 13

She woke up drenched in sweat, even though her lair was cool. It was late. She imagined that by now the quarter-moon was high in the night sky. She was irritated that she had fallen asleep, when she should have been reviewing her plans and checking her equipment.

She was disturbed by the recurring nightmare. The despair and emptiness that enveloped her when she had learned about her father's deadly construction accident continued to embrace her. The fury she felt the day she lost her brother was still with her. She constantly played the scenes over in her head. They never left her.

Tonight's activity will be comforting.

She threw her feet over the edge of her cot and flipped on the master switch to the transformer that regulated power through the underground bunker. She heard the Honda generator belch as it kicked-in. The lights in the dark tunnels of her home drank the electricity and brightened, illuminating a chaotic but organized assortment of equipment, furniture, boxes, shelves and closets. Her hideout was comfortable and provided all of the necessities for her to thrive, but it was not furnished in luxury nor did it bare any semblance to a 21st-century home. It resembled a storage facility, sometimes used as an office, which is exactly what it was supposed to look like.

She had purchased three interconnecting WWII-era munitions tunnels more than twenty years ago from Paul Savio. Each tunnel was about twenty feet wide with fifteen to twenty foot tall ceilings, and stretched at least two hundred feet into the bowels of the mountain. Savio was a local landowner and real estate investor happy to unload the undesirable holdings to the local girl for a good price. The tunnels, located deep within the Waikele Gulch made a some

71

perfect respite and staging place for her and her small group of trusted soldiers. The location was off the grid and far from the prying eyes of the government or curious passersby. She felt safe here.

Two weeks after closing the sale, Mr. Savio's house was robbed and vandalized by the same pleasant looking local woman from whom he had so easily profited. It had been one of her first major heists, and an important confirmation of her life's work. She recouped 75% of the price she had paid for her new home by selling the jewelry, artwork and artifacts she had recovered from Savio. The cash she found in his safe was used for operating expenses and she began the tradition of making anonymous cash contributions to small local charities. She didn't imagine herself to be a modern day Robin Hood, but she did believe that the wealth of the few needed to be redistributed.

The profit and altruism was secondary. Her main purpose was to punish the largest and wealthiest landowners and businesses in the islands—the families and institutions that had profited most from stealing the ceded lands from the Hawaiian people, and that had brought down the legitimate Kingdom. She sought retribution from the descendents of the families that she blamed for the extinction of the ancient Hawaiian culture and values. They had given smallpox, measles, diabetes and countless other maladies to the natives. The population of native Hawaiians had dropped from hundreds of thousands to mere ten thousands within a few decades.

With a missionary zeal unlike any other, they had turned the indigenous tribes away from the land and nature. The missionaries outlawed the native language, traditions, even *Hula.*[15] Christianity became the status quo. The mostly white owned plantations, developers and businesses, always

---

[15] Hawaiian traditional dance

looking towards profit rather than balanced sustainability, introduced invasive species of plants and animals that soon overwhelmed the islands' fragile ecosystem. Asphalt and concrete scoured the land, making the ocean brown and muddy with agricultural waste and storm runoff. By the time her grandfather had been born, the mid-20th century, the Hawaiian people and their way of life were near extinction.

They deserve to pay. They must be reminded.

She made three or four selective visits per year to the offices or homes of these well-known local families. She picked the family or the business that had most recently captured the accolades of the local press, or who had posted unusually high profits for the quarter. The establishments she visited were a proverbial "who's who" of local high society— Atherton, Bishop, Baldwin, Castle, Cook, Case, Campbell, Dillingham, Dole, Kaiser, Parker, Steiner, and Ward. She also made a point to visit the trustees of Bishop Estates, Queen Liliuokalani Trust, and Kamehameha Schools—even though they mostly did good work, she felt they deserved frequent reminders of their complacency and role in the downfall of her people.

Soon after the HPD and FBI finally came to the conclusion that it was the same criminal who was terrorizing the wealthiest and most powerful families in the state, the Honolulu Advertiser had christened her "The Mongoose." She still had the newspaper clipping pinned to the wall next to her computer.

October 12, 2001– The Mongoose strikes again!

For the last four years, Hawaii's wealthiest and most influential families have lived in fear. Targeted by a clever and vicious vandal and thief, their homes and lives have been repeatedly violated. The latest victims, the Case family of AOL, Punahou School, and local political fame, had their

73

ancestral Manoa Valley home broken into Saturday night. The thief reportedly removed a small fortune of cash, precious documents, artifacts and jewelry from the home. Most disturbingly, the perpetrator vandalized and defaced irreplaceable family photographs, portraits, heirloom furniture and other treasures.

Senator Edward Case said afterwards, "The jewelry, cash and other things stolen are replaceable. What we don't understand is the violent destruction of our personal family treasures. There is no value in destroying photographs, portraits and furniture. It seems like the vandal or vandals just wanted to punish us in some way."

Over the last four years, twelve prominent local families on all islands have been victimized in a similar fashion. HPD, State Police and the FBI have few clues. According to Detective David Morimoto, they have no fingerprints or other physical evidence to help with their investigation. Video surveillance at a few of the targeted homes captured shadowy images of a person breaking into the property, but there are no strong leads in this ongoing investigation.

"The thief is clever and quick. He targets his victims carefully and inflicts maximum damage. He strikes only when the homes are vacant and is able to circumvent all surveillance and security systems with ease. The break-ins occur usually just before dawn or just after dusk. He seems to be most active at these times, just like a mongoose."

Unofficially, this menace is now being referred to as "The Mongoose." Authorities are asking pawnshops and online shoppers to be on the lookout for suspicious jewelry and artifacts proffered up for sale that may have been from one of these robberies. The public is asked to call Crime Stoppers if they have any information.

She smiled at the thought that even after all of these years, they still suspected she was a man. HPD, State Police and the FBI were no closer to finding her. They had all but given up, telling the powerful families in the islands to beef up their security and keep their valuables in safe deposit boxes. The political uproar was amusing to watch, and the pathetic attempts the authorities made to catch her scent were laughable.

She hated the nickname "the Mongoose," but it did seem somewhat fitting. The mongoose was an invasive species introduced by the white man to solve the problem of the exploding rat population on the islands. The effort failed miserably—there was plenty of indigenous food for the mongoose. The mongoose and the rats thrived. Native species of birds and insects rapidly declined, rodent borne diseases continued to spread. The government tried to eradicate the clever weasels, but they gave up and eventually the mongoose became a common and accepted sight throughout the islands.

Maggie felt that it was fitting that the namesake the press and HPD had given her was crafty, clever and troublesome—a thorn in the side of the white man's carelessness. The mongoose should be a reminder to leave nature alone and respect the balance between the ocean, forest and mountains. However, being associated with the invasive species left a bad taste in her mouth. She vowed to step up her work, to make them pay, and to continue to punish them as long as she could.

As she made her final preparations for the evening, she felt confident. Only James Spencer and his lackey, Lou Costelilia, had any hint of her trail, and she was sure that after the events of the last 48 hours and the encrypted message she had sent Spencer, that he would back off. If not, she could always escalate her efforts to dissuade him further.

Her work for the people was more important than any faded memories of their time together as teenagers.

The ride to Black Point was pleasant and traffic free. Her driver slowed the black Mercedes SUV and made two deliberate loops of Kaikoo Place before stopping fifty feet or so west of the driveway to the Dillingham house.

"Everything looks quiet," he said. "Security doesn't make their next round until 5:15."

The Mongoose made one last check of her equipment, zipped up her black jumpsuit, and made a final adjustment to the laces of her black boots.

"Time check. 4:37 AM."

"Yes, ma'am."

"Be here at exactly 5:03."

That would give her exactly twenty-six minutes, more than enough time. She set her wrist alarm on vibrate, slipped on her backpack and disappeared into the bushes alongside the road. The SUV drove away silently.

She followed the wall to the edge of the Dillingham property, staying in the shadows of the bushes and trees, away from the landscape lighting and motion detectors. The steep driveway turned sharply towards the ocean. She stopped and listened. The only sound she heard were the rhythmic waves crashing against the volcanic cliffs of Black Point. Nothing moved. The quarter moon and landscape lighting gave up just enough light for her to see clearly, but not enough to reveal her presence.

She threw the grappling hook over the eight-foot high cement wall. The black nylon rope slipped loosely through her gloved hands. She pulled the hook tight until it was secured, then she easily scaled the wall. She landed silently within a plethora of tropical flowers and bushes in the front garden of the estate. She reeled in the rope, collapsed the hook and placed everything neatly in her backpack. Nothing was ever wasted or left behind.

She took out her favorite piece of equipment, a compact and extendable "Helping Hand Gripper" that she had purchased on QVC. She had modified the novelty item, originally made to help disabled persons, or housewives, reach high places in their kitchens, to operate a small can of black spray paint and wire cutters. She smiled at how such a simple device allowed a short, five-foot-two Hawaiian-Asian woman reach over twenty feet. She moved deliberately underneath each of the surveillance cameras and motion sensors. She knew exactly where each was located. The cameras were blocked with the black paint, while the motion sensor wires were deftly cut.

She crouched underneath a stained glass window, and took a short breather. She put the gripper away and took out her glass cutting tools. She could've gone through the front door, but that would require her to rush quickly to the central alarm system in the kitchen. Going through the window was a little more difficult, but less stressful. Once inside the house, she could disarm the central alarm system at her leisure.

In less than a minute, she squeezed through the hole in the glass and dropped silently onto the hardwood floor. She checked her watch.

4:42 AM, still plenty of time.

From the side pocket of her backpack, she took out an expandable black duffel bag. As she moved efficiently through the house, she began to fill it with the most valuable knickknacks and artifacts—an antique silver tea set, Koa wood bowls, small bronze statues, antique clocks, Chinese ceramics, carved ivory, Tapa cloth hangings, a feather lei, and anything else that looked valuable and could fit into her bag. She made her way to the kitchen and easily disarmed the alarm system. Then she went to the library where she knew the patriarch's safe was located behind a family portrait.

Two and a half minutes later the contents of the safe were transferred to her possession. She continued through the house filling up her duffel bag like an anti-Santa. Her wrist alarm vibrated.

4:50 AM, now the fun part.

She placed her now full duffel bag next to the front door. She removed two very important tools from her backpack: a modified 6-pound sledgehammer and a 12-inch customized straight razor blade. For the next ten minutes, the Mongoose ripped and smashed her way through the house, causing maximum mayhem and damage. What couldn't be slashed with her razor blade was crushed with the sledgehammer. Everything within reach succumbed to her tornado of destruction. She targeted family portraits, priceless artwork and antique furniture in particular.

She went through each room of the house. Priceless Tiffany lamp shades in the library were decapitated. Luxurious leather couches and chairs were disemboweled. Shelves of first edition books had their spines severed. Antique tables and chairs in the dining room were dismembered. Ming Dynasty porcelain vases, bowls, and plates were shattered into thousands of pieces. Every piece of glass and crystal met the same fate. In the living room, the frames of family portraits and photographs were splintered and special attention was given to the slicing of the images they contained—the blood of memories spilled onto the floor.

For a tiny woman the extent of the damage she caused was extraordinary. The pure satisfaction that she gained from the exertion of energy brought a huge smile to her face and quiet laughter to her throat. Her desire for revenge and her need to punish drove her. For the Mongoose this ten minutes of violent exercise was better than sex, better than a gourmet dinner or the high from a hit of meth she had learned to love during her Chinatown years.

Her wrist alarm vibrated.

5 AM, it's time to go.

She smashed a one hundred-year-old Wicker rocking chair in the living room for good measure. She looked around to make sure that everything was to her satisfaction, then bolted out the front door and dashed up the driveway. She stayed in the shadows until the black SUV made a loop through Kaikoo Place.

5:03 AM, my ride is here. Right on schedule.

She rested contentedly in the plush black leather seats of the vehicle. She was exhausted, but almost giddy with relief. Satisfaction coursed through her veins. She laid her head on top of the burgeoning duffel bag and drifted off to sleep. The driver woke her up when they arrived at her lair.

Chapter 14

Officers Grant and Suzuki disliked being in the middle of the abandoned sugar cane fields. The unpaved access road was potholed and rugged. The red earth cracked as it baked under the unforgiving tropical sun. It hadn't rained more than a sprinkle on this part of the Leeward side of the island for several weeks. The sugarcane, wilted and overgrown, should have been harvested months ago. The fields, instead of reflecting the deep green promise of raw sugar, projected a brown and dusty death.

They pulled in front of the Waianae Sugar Mill. Grant slammed on the brakes and the patrol car slid to a stop. The cloud of red dust that had been following them silently enveloped the car. It took a minute for the dust to settle, and the clear blue sky to reveal itself through the dirty windshield. Grant turned on the wipers and added a few squirts of soapy water. The dust turned blood red and ran down the sides of the dirty patrol cruiser. It only made visibility worse.

"Damn, looks hot out there," Suzuki said taking a swig of bottled water.

"Not a breath of wind. Not one cloud in the sky," Grant said looking out the window. "It would be nice to be assigned to the Windward side every once in a while."

"Sure, then we could complain about the rain."

"Anything on the scanner?"

"Not yet," Suzuki said. "Pull up a little closer to the side of the main building."

The Wi-Fi scanner pinged.

"We got a hit!"

"—sure it's the right frequency?"

"Yeah, I'll call it in," Suzuki said.

Grant turned off the engine and popped the trunk. He waited until his partner informed the dispatcher and requested backup.

"Let's do it," Grant said.

The two police officers stepped out of their air-conditioned patrol car into the overwhelming heat and humidity of the Leeward plains. They hesitated just for a moment as their bodies adjusted to the new, harsher environment. Grant felt the heat from the red earth singe the bottom of his boots. Suzuki took the last swig of water from this plastic bottle and tossed it into the trunk. They put on their flak jackets, helmets, goggles, and checked their equipment. Suzuki took the Remington shotgun. Grant checked the clip on his Glock 22.

"Test audio," Grant said.

"10–4, I can hear you loud and clear," Suzuki replied.

Guns ready, Grant led the way to the front door of the main building. There was nothing but red earth, brown sugarcane, and the occasional piece of rusted farm equipment surrounding the building. Everything of value had been pilfered long ago. The door was open. Most of the windows were broken. They laid their backs against the wall of the building. The cemented volcanic rock reflected a hint of coolness. The officers peered inside.

The once flourishing sugar mill was now completely empty. Every bit of scrap metal, wire and usable wood had been removed. Rats and cockroaches now inhabited the building that was once the economic foundation of the Leeward community. Grant covered Suzuki as he slipped into the main room.

"All clear," Suzuki said.

"Roger."

They moved carefully through the first floor of the building.

"I got footprints," Grant said.

"They look fresh," Suzuki replied, coming up behind his partner.

They followed the footprints to a door that apparently led to the basement. The door was locked.

"How far out is backup?"

"Probably another fifteen minutes," Suzuki said looking at his watch.

"I'm not in the mood for waiting," Grant said. "Are you?"

"Nope."

Grant stepped back and with one blow of his large black boot smashed the door off its hinges. Both men crouched low and waited until the noise of breaking lumber subsided. A dusty silence reclaimed the structure. A strong sour, sticky sweet odor came wafting through the basement door.

"I smell flowers," Suzuki said.

"Ginger, I believe," Grant replied. "Ready?"

Lou heard the men above him. When the basement door was kicked in, he knew that the police had arrived. He was elated, or at least he should have been. He didn't think he would've lasted much longer, but something was nagging at the back of his consciousness, and it wasn't the pain or the loss of his implants. He felt something deep in his gut, a primal instinct that told him there was danger. He had felt the same thing on several occasions during deployment, usually just before an IED exploded or insurgents attacked. He had learned to follow his instincts. He tried to warn the police, but his mouth was duct taped. All he could do was mumble incoherently.

The men came down the staircase. Hearing the moaning spurred them on.

Lou looked around the room, as far as his neck would allow him. Everything seemed the same as it was earlier in the day. The vases full of Ginger were still the only odd features within sight. The flowers were dead, wilting and brown. The fragrance was no longer pleasant or complex, instead they gave off a dull uncomfortable fermented smell.

Costelilia," one of the officers said. "Is that you?"

He grunted in return, and shook his head vigorously.

"HPD!" Suzuki shouted

Lou fixed his gaze straight ahead. Suddenly, he recognized something odd about the vases. The stalks of the Ginger were stuck into a pliable gray plastic. It looked like clay.

Plastic explosives! Lou screamed inside his head.

He tried again to warn the officers. They needed to stay back, but it was too late. They couldn't understand his muffled vocalizations, darting eyes or shaking head. They thought he was desperate to be rescued. The officers checked the perimeter of the room and then moved towards him.

He hated the helplessness more than the violent explosion that he knew was coming. He had been in this position too many times before. He had seen too many good soldiers die because he couldn't warn them soon enough. He hoped that this time he would just die with them.

The officers stepped in to the perimeter created by the Ginger flowers.

The infrared trigger connecting all twelve vases fired each of the plastic explosive devices within nano-seconds of each other. The result was one sustained explosion that ripped through the entire basement. The sound was deafening. The shockwave took the air out of the room. Shards of glass, Ginger stalks and flower petals flew to every corner, slamming into the cement walls, wooden beams and ceiling. The neatly stacked bamboo poles were shredded by the blast.

The Mongoose had designed the IED to disorient, shock, and maim—not kill. It worked perfectly. Most of the glass shrapnel was projected upwards and out towards the perimeter. Glass sliced through the officers' protective clothing like razors through butter. Veins and arteries were severed, but no lives were lost. Lou once again suffered a concussion, and a few minor cuts from the glass. Ginger petals lodged themselves into his chest, neck, cheeks and forehead. He heard one of the officers call for help.

"Explosion – Officer down!"

Lou heard sirens in the distance as he slipped into a blissful unconsciousness.

Chapter 15

"Officer down... Send EMS."

James listened to the action unfold on the HPD scanner. He tapped into the dashboard video camera on the patrol car parked in front of the sugar mill. He saw the windows of the basement had been blown out. Smoke and dust billowed from the red dirt stained building. He could hear the officers groaning in pain. He heard sirens in the background.

He was angry, distraught, frustrated and emotionally drained.

At first, James had been relieved that the patrol officers had picked up Lou's microwave frequency. He had listened carefully while the officers entered the abandoned building. He was thrilled that Lou had been found, but frustrated that he couldn't play a more active role. He could only watch and listen.

He hoped that Lou was alive and he would recover quickly from whatever ordeal he had suffered, but this turn of events had been totally unexpected. The sound of the explosion had come rushing through his speakers, the shockwave knocking the euphoria from him like a sucker punch to the gut. A silent dread took its place.

Why the sudden change? Why was this message so personal and close to home?

James made a conscious effort to take his eyes off the video screen and struggled to tune out the voices and sirens. He tried to focus on the encrypted message he had received embedded in the photograph from his past. It had explicitly given the impression that Lou's life was to be spared— backing away from his consultant work with HPD was a no-brainer if it meant the safety of his best friend.

It wasn't supposed to end this way.

James still had no clue who had sent it. With upgraded Internet search and analytics software he'd recently received, he had been tracking the photograph through its life on the Internet for most of the afternoon. It had been sent and resent through several of the most popular social media networks—Facebook, Tumblr and Instagram. Literally thousands of people had had access to the photograph. Anyone with the most rudimentary understanding of Photoshop could have manipulated the image and embedded the message.

He had created an algorithm that was checking through each contact to see if they had Photoshop knowledge or any connection to Lou, the HPD, or himself. There were already eight hundred names on the list. He would narrow the search with additional variables, but he felt that there wasn't any real chance of pinpointing the suspect. Nevertheless, he wouldn't give up. He had learned that even the most unlikely lead could break a case wide open.

"Two officers and one civilian in the basement," a police officer reported to the dispatcher. "All three injured, but still breathing. EMS on the scene."

James took a deep breath. His ventilator responded, giving him the extra inspiratory pressure. He wanted to jump for joy and punch his fists into the air. All he could manage was a muffled yell.

Lou is alive!

Lillian rushed in to the room.

"Are you okay, Mister Spencer?"

"Yes, yes, everything is just great!"

"Are you sure? You look tired."

"I'm okay Lillian," he said. Then, in order to give her something to do, he asked, "May I have some iced tea?"

As usual, he had kept his business with the HPD from Lillian. He never discussed his work with her. He felt that it was better that way—less complicated for both of them. He had not told her that Lou was missing. However, from her broad smile and quick steps exiting the room, James suspected she had overheard much of the events of the last two days.

"Sweet iced tea, coming right up!"

He watched from the patrol car dashboard video camera as more police officers and detectives swarmed into the area. His perspective was restricted to one angle and the images were grainy, but it was something. He continued to listen to the officers as they communicated with each other and secured the premises.

The audio was one-way and interrupted with static. This type of surveillance was adequate, but nowhere near as comprehensive and satisfying as when he was connected neurologically with Lou. With Lou as his sensory receptor and the 3-D holographic grid in his control-workroom, he was able to live the experience, not just passively watch or listen.

God, he has to be alive.

He saw detective Morimoto's sedan pull up. The slim well-dressed detective issued several orders and then went into the sugar mill. A few minutes later, James watched three stretchers being loaded into the awaiting ambulances. They were on their way to Queen's Hospital. James Skyped the detective's cell phone.

"Morimoto here," the detective answered. James saw him standing by the front door of the sugar mill.

"Detective, tell me how Lou and the officers are doing."

"Suzuki is in fair condition, with a concussion from the blast and a few cuts and bruises. Grant is stable, but serious. Glass cut through the artery in his left leg. He's lost a lot of blood. Most of the shrapnel missed your friend

Costelilia, but he's still unconscious. It looks like he's suffered quite a beating and is severely dehydrated."

"Thank you Detective."

"I've got my boys going through the sugar mill, but I doubt they will find very much."

Morimoto sounded bored.

"You mentioned glass. Where did that come from?" James asked.

"From what Suzuki has told us, there were at least a dozen glass vases circling Costelilia. It seems that the vases were the IEDs. No word yet on how they were triggered."

"That seems odd. A glass vase doesn't seem like your typical container for an explosive device."

"I agree, Spencer. But, who the hell knows, there's lots of craziness out here. I gave up being surprised long ago. The flowers in the vases were Ginger. Does that mean anything to you?"

"No, not at the moment," James lied. "You can bet I'll look into it tho...– though." His voice cracked.

The Ginger was the key.

Where was that iced tea?

"Okay then, been a busy day. I'll keep you posted if we find anything here," Detective Morimoto said.

There was an awkward moment of silence, then Morimoto asked, "Any news on the Mongoose case?"

The detective noticed a long pause before Spencer answered.

"No," he lied again. "I'm going through the photographs and other reports you sent to me this morning. Looks like the same MO. The vandalism is escalating."

"Yeah he's pissed all right," Morimoto said.

"Okay, back to work. Thanks detective."

"Sure," Morimoto ended the call thinking, '*Fuckin amateur, he's definitely withholding something...*'

Chapter 16

The meeting took place in a private room at the exclusive Pacific Club in downtown Honolulu. Much of the Island's business had been conducted on the elegant premises for the last 160 years. The establishment is known as the oldest private club in the United States west of the Mississippi. The five patriarchs of some of the wealthiest, powerful and most well-known Hawaiian families relaxed and enjoyed idle chit-chat after a light lunch consisting of broiled fresh-caught mahi-mahi, garlic mashed Wailua potatoes, creamed baby spinach, and a fresh island salad.

The men represented a perfect cross-section of Hawaiian power and land ownership that had surfaced during the post World War II era. They were struggling to retain that power during the 21st century, and to that end, they had created an unofficial, but mutually beneficial council that controlled most of the business on the islands. They sat at the table speaking for their families, partners, business associates and constituents.

Two of the members were haoles, prominent leaders of the old-money plantation and missionary families. They sat at opposite ends of the table. They were slim and white haired, comfortable in the plush surroundings. One gentleman was Japanese-American. A *nisei*,[16] born on a Maui sugar plantation. He served his country valiantly in the war, became an attorney and was now a leader of the State's Democratic political machine. He had a habit of constantly cleaning his wire rim glasses. Across from him, a Chinese man sat sipping hot tea. He'd also been born and raised on a plantation, but instead of pursuing military service and higher education, he had become a powerful merchant and

---

[16] Second generation Japanese

successful real estate investor. The fifth man was native Hawaiian. He was from the island of Hawaii. He was a ranch owner and visibly uncomfortable wearing a jacket and tie—required by the Pacific Club dress code.

The waiters cleared the table and retreated, allowing the men their privacy.

"It's time we rid ourselves of this nuisance," the eldest of the patriarchs said from the end of the table closest to the garden. He had called the group together.

"We all agree," the Japanese man said.

"HPD is clueless, and the FBI really doesn't give a damn," the Chinese patriarch added.

"It's time to take action, to protect ourselves and our families."

"The last attack at the Dillingham mansion was especially vicious. It seems like our weasel is getting bolder," the man from Hawaii Island said.

"Does everyone agree then?" the leader of the group asked.

"Aye," a couple of the men responded.

"Yes, we wouldn't be here otherwise," the Japanese man said, slightly irritated.

Everyone nodded.

"Then, we shall proceed."

Chapter 17

Getting out of the penthouse apartment and traveling any distance was not an easy endeavor for James and his caregivers. He only took excursions with Lou and Lillian, and then just for short trips to the clinic, beach or the mall. He was much more comfortable in his apartment. Traveling and being in public exhausted what little energy he had. He didn't like crowds or traffic. He wasn't social. He didn't like the stares he got from curious children and the seemingly constant stream of born-again Christians who liked to pray over him. He never refused their prayers, but it annoyed him that they assumed he was a Christian and more often than not, without inquiry, they believed he was a war veteran. Out of politeness, he let them do their thing and gave short answers to their questions. Lou usually stepped off to the side, excusing himself from the spectacle. At least the prayers made Lillian feel better.

Lillian had to contact one of her friends, Pablo, to help on this excursion since Lou was not available. Lou usually took care of most of the transfers and he drove the van. Pablo was a competent nurse and James had used him on many occasions. He was a happy and talkative Filipino man. Lillian enjoyed his company. They chatted incessantly about relatives and neighborhood scandals while safely transporting James to Queen's hospital where Lou was recovering.

It was time for them to have a face-to-face conversation—Skype would not do.

On the way to the hospital, James replayed his conversations with detective Morimoto over the last couple of days in his head. With his near photographic memory, he flipped through the documents, reports, spreadsheets, e-mails, photographs and videos that he had compiled regarding Lou's assault and the Mongoose case. It all made sense.

Lou's kidnapping was linked to the Mongoose case.

He was grateful to the detective and the officers of HPD. They had done a super-job finding Lou. His buddy was okay. This was great news, yet he was feeling anxious about the new revelations that had been uncovered. He didn't like lying to Morimoto, but as soon as he realized that the explosives in the basement at the sugar mill were housed in vases containing Ginger, he had connected the dots. Lying to Lou was worse. He had to tell the truth.

James absently watched the busy streets of Honolulu pass by while tracing the threads of evidence through the compartments of his orderly brain. He was not surprised how everything had fallen into place. Solving the Mongoose case had been a private obsession ever since the Spencer family home had been hit six years ago. No one knew he had been working the case. The Mongoose was his own private "white whale." And now, he knew the answer.

He had come close to the conclusion a few months earlier—the Mongoose was Maggie, his friend from high school—Mae-Linh Malia Nguyen Kawanakapili. At the time, all he had was a strong gut feeling and circumstantial evidence, but he was getting closer to the hard evidence he needed. She must have felt his scent on her trail. That's why she had sent the messages warning him to back off. He had received the first embedded message about two years ago. The first few had been vague, but they had progressively gotten more specific and ominous. The most recent was the most personal and telling. She had made a mistake by using a photograph from their shared past.

Then there was the timing of Lou's kidnapping, and the beating he suffered from green bamboo—the same type of bamboo they had played under at Jackass Ginger Falls. He

96

still smelled the flowers anonymously delivered to his apartment and relived the memories they brought with them. He thought about the Ginger laced IEDs that miraculously didn't kill, but just inflicted flesh wounds. These were all just additional warnings. Everything added up. He knew the identity of the Mongoose. It was clear that her threats were meant to be taken seriously.

Maggie was the Mongoose.

James shivered. It was time to come clean with Lou. He would be angry that he hadn't been informed earlier. He would be sad to know that Maggie was behind the events of the last few days and the so-called Mongoose burglaries.

James stopped by officers Suzuki and Grant's rooms to pay his respects before visiting Lou. The officers were doing well and would soon be back on the job. They had heard of Doctor Spencer, Lou Costelilia's bed-ridden partner. They appreciated his gesture, but the patrol officers were not that impressed with the man in the wheelchair. James was not an imposing figure or a great conversationalist. He didn't mind that the men showed little interest in his presence or words. He was used to dealing with wounded soldiers that had much more important things to worry about than being polite to a stranger. His visit was short, the anonymous donations James made to the officers' families were enough, and would speak volumes.

Visiting with Lou was a completely different scenario. Lou and James had a bond that had been forged in high school and had been cemented throughout their adult lives. The last twelve years had brought them even closer. Lou understood James' physical limitations and fully appreciated his mental acuity. They were able to have long and meaningful conversations when needed. When they talked, Lou listened carefully to each softly uttered word and halting phrase. He matched James' rhythm and pace, pausing to rest and breathe between thoughts. Their conversations were never rushed.

James, on the other hand, enjoyed Lou's energy and sense of humor. He encouraged his best friend to engage him in stories and jokes garnered from the depths of life his experiences. James asked broad, open-ended questions. He marveled at the answers. He gladly listened to his friend for hours on end, never wavering even if he had heard the same story several times over. If he was tired, James would just close his eyes and let the words wash over him. Lou didn't ever seem to mind, an attentive audience wasn't always necessary, he knew his buddy was listening. Lou was the brother that James always wanted. He loved him unconditionally and was grateful for his companionship.

James eyes welled up with tears when Lou shouted an obscenity-laced greeting as he was wheeled into the private room. He laughed when Lou quickly apologized to Lillian for his foul language. Lou plowed forward while James tried to catch his breath.

"Lillian, you look just as lovely as ever."

Before she could recover from blushing and respond, Lou continued.

"Pablo, my man, looking good! How's the family?"

"Everybody's good. You're looking very well," Pablo said.

"I'm doing just great. The meds are good. The nurses are better, and now my favorite doctor has come for a visit!" Lou said, as he lifted himself just a little bit taller in the bed.

He winced from the pain he felt. It was clearly visible to his visitors.

"Doctor Spencer, can you do something about this headache?"

Lillian wiped the moisture from James' eyes and directed Pablo to move him closer to the bedside. James, still unable to speak or catch his breath, nodded his thanks to Lillian and fixed his eyes on Lou.

"Something tells me we have to have a conversation," Lou said. "Lillian, how about some hot chocolate from the cafeteria? The pork adobo is pretty good too, Pablo. The good Doctor and I will be okay for a while. If he goes into cardiac arrest, I promise to call the nurses."

James nodded to Lillian that they should be left alone.

Lou waved to Lillian and Pablo as they closed the door. He waited.

"Lou, I'm sorry," James finally said.

"Sorry for nothing. I'm the idiot that let some thugs smash me in the back of the head."

"I should've seen it coming."

"Nonsense. Let's get on with it, what's going on?"

James was not sure where to start. He had to tell Lou about Maggie, and they had to discuss the implants. He decided to begin with the easy topic.

"How are you feeling?" James lapsed into his best physician's bedside manner.

"Okay, we can deal with the medical stuff first," Lou said laughing. "The bruises are healing. Nothing's broken. My head hurts like hell though."

"We need to replace the implants."

"Both of them?"

"That's up to you."

"Really? You mean I have the choice to turn off the irritating voice in my head."

"Yes Lou. I can just replace the implant that regulates your brain activity," James said taking a long breath. "You would be back to normal in a couple of weeks."

"That's reassuring. But, come on man, don't you have something new and better to offer. I mean, these implants were several years old already. Where's all the new technology you're always talking about?"

"Of course, the new implant would be an upgrade. Without getting too technical, it would be smaller and offer at least twenty times more neural capacity."

"I will be twenty times smarter?" Lou asked. Without waiting for an answer he said, "I'm in."

"I don't know about smarter, but you should have way less PTSD symptoms and literally millions more synapse connections," James replied. "We'll have to see how much difference there really is."

"What about the other thing?"

"It's also smaller and upgraded. Same basic functionality, but improved reception and transmission quality," James took a moment to synchronize his breath with his portable ventilator. "More flexibility for tweaking the interface software on the fly, without total shut down."

"That sounds like the mechanic fixing the car while it's driving full speed down the autobahn."

"Good analogy," James said. "I promise I'd let you know before I switched out the transmission."

"That's good to know."

Lou squinted, pretending to think deeply about the proposition.

"Okay let's do it. I'm too accustomed to having you inside my head to turn you off now."

"Great, I'll schedule the surgery."

"Not too quick, Herr Doctor. I want to be able to disconnect from my head. No more double passwords," Lou said. "No more Spencer protocol to say good night. I want a simple on or off switch."

This disturbed James. However, it was not unsuspected and not unreasonable. Lou had been complaining about the lack of privacy for a while.

"Our login and logout protocol is to protect you, and the system."

"Yep, I know all that. Fix it or the deal is off."

James knew that his friend was serious. It was possible to set up, but it left the door open to unseen vulnerabilities.

"If you switch off, I'll be completely in the dark. They'll be no way for me to know what is going on."

"Exactly," Lou said looking directly into his eyes. "Deal or no deal?"

James didn't like it. He didn't like the dark undertone he sensed in Lou's voice, but there was no alternative. He had to agree.

"Deal."

"I'd shake hands with you, but I know your grip is a little light these days," Lou said. "Anything else doctor?"

"I'd like to replace the battery pack in your shoulder while we're at it," he replied, breathing easier. "Also smaller, and with some additional backup transmission capabilities."

"No problem, hack away."

"And, a protective plate over the implants. Just in case you get another nasty blow to your skull."

"I don't want a metal plate in my head," Lou said. "Just think of the fun TSA would have with me. I already set off all of their alarms."

"It's not metal. A new alloy-grade plastic. Kind of like Kevlar, but stronger and lighter."

"Sounds cool."

Lou reached over and gave his buddy a slight pat to his chest.

"You doing the surgery?"

"Nope, Doctors Mott-Smith and Gordon will do the honors. I'll be watching."

"Let's roll," Lou said smiling broadly. "Now what's really bothering you?"

James appreciated his friend's insight.

They sat in the hospital room in silence. Lou gazed down at his wheelchair-bound motionless friend. The irony of the situation did not elude either one of them—one of the world's most prominent neurosurgeons was suffering from a terminal neurological disease. He had saved countless lives in emergency rooms throughout the world. He had dedicated millions of dollars and devoted the last fifteen years to improving the lives of thousands of soldiers returning from war with PTSD and TBI. And yet, he had basically ignored his own diagnosis.

Many in the field felt that he should use his incredible experience and resources to find a treatment or cure for ALS, but James had no interest in researching his own disease. He believed it was a natural occurrence, a rare mutation devastating in its totality, but benign in origin. Head trauma was not a natural phenomenon. It was worth fighting. It could not be cured, but it could be healed. He had no illusions that he could fix every man-inflicted injury to the brain, but at least he didn't feel he was struggling against millions of years of natural selection, God, destiny or some greater universal power.

"It's Maggie," James finally said.

Chapter 18

Michael "Hammerhead" Kalani Jefferson, the undisputed boss of Honolulu's largest organized crime syndicate was surprised when Chinn Ho Lin, a respectable Oahu real estate investor contacted him with an unusual proposition. Lin, claiming to represent the big families of Hawaii, offered him a handsome sum to find and eliminate the so-called Mongoose.

At first Jefferson wasn't that interested, he had plenty of income and a thriving organization to run. Also, on more than one occasion, artifacts and jewelry had come across his desk that he knew had probably originated from the Mongoose's exploits. Why plug a perfectly good pipeline?

When Lin sweetened the pot by saying that Jefferson could have first rights to the significant wealth rumored to be stashed in the Mongoose's hideout, he agreed.

With gangland efficiency, Jefferson's deputies soon knew everything the HPD and FBI knew—which wasn't much. His men quickly cut through the rumors about the Mongoose. They strong-armed local alliances and sources for solid information and determined that Doctor James Spencer, a neurologist and HPD consultant, had the information that they needed. Finding the reclusive Spencer was time consuming, but not that difficult.

A few days later, the Akamai air-conditioning van pulled into the loading zone of the Nuuanu Valley luxury condominium. Three large Polynesian men in dirty overalls climbed out. Two of the men stayed by the van and enjoyed a much needed smoke break. The security guard noted that they look tired.

"Akamai, here to install air conditioner for apartment 2130. Mrs. Phong," the driver said, leaning heavily on the security desk.

"Looks like you've had a long day."

"We sure have, bradda. Last stop for us, and then it's *pau hana.*[17] Nothing but beer and good *grinds* for the weekend."

"I hear ya," the haole security guard replied, happy to be called a brother by a local.

He checked the register and noted that Mrs. Phong had filed the proper request to allow the workers into her apartment. Protocol required that he stay with them while they did their work—that would be no problem, the night watch would arrive soon.

"Looks like everything's okay," the security guard said. "I need to make a call and a quick loop around the perimeter, then I can take you upstairs."

"Right on, bradda. Gives us a few minutes to finish-up our *ono* plate lunch from Graces' Diner and get our gear together."

"Ah, Graces' is da best. You get kalbi?" the guard said, trying his best to sound local.

"Course," the Polynesian man said smiling. "Where's my manners, you like some grinds?"

"Sure!"

A short fifteen minutes later, the security guard was letting the three men into apartment 2130. He sat down in the living room and began to relish the delicious local style plate lunch—a three-pound plate of starch, pickled vegetables and protein. It easily rivaled any sandwich or lunch he had enjoyed in his hometown of Atlantic City.

The two scoops rice and two scoops macaroni salad he found to be a little bit excessive, but the sweet, spicy taste of the barbecued pork and chicken were phenomenal. Each week that passed made him feel more at home in these

---

[17] Work is done

islands. One day, he imagined he would feel like a true *Kamaania.*[18]

"We come in and out for the next hour, das okay with you?" one of the AC men asked. "Got three new AC. Lots a boxes, equipment and *da kine.*[19]"

"No problem, bra, just keep the door propped open," the white security guard said.

Stupid haole, talk to them in pidgin and give them some local food, and they like little puppies willing to do just about anything, the *Akamai*[20] man thought to himself.

Two men busied themselves installing the air conditioners for apartment 2130. The third man discreetly entered the stairwell and hiked up to the penthouse floor. He moved slowly and carefully. He knew the apartment would be wired. He had plenty of time. They knew that Spencer and his caregivers were out visiting Queen's Hospital.

He was an expert at breaking and entering, bypassing alarm systems, and retrieving hard to find items or electronic data. His services did not come cheap, but for this particular job he'd accepted Jefferson's first offer. He was well aware of the Mongoose's reputation and relished the opportunity to stop him. One less expert thief operating in the islands could only enhance his status.

After entering and disabling all of the alarm systems, motion sensors and closed-circuit video cameras—there were several of them throughout the apartment. He began to look for anything, paper, photograph or electronic file, that might give clues as to the identity of the Mongoose. He didn't rush. The two security guards were more than occupied.

The first idiot guard that had let them into the condominium was enjoying his plate lunch by now, and

---

[18] Local people
[19] The thing, stuff, what ever
[20] Smart

would soon be lulled into a full-on *kanak attack*.[21] A lovely Thai exotic dancer, who was presumably waiting for her girlfriend, was entertaining the second guard in the security office. She would buzz the men as soon as Spencer returned from his outing.

He started rifling through the filing cabinets and storage boxes stacked against the walls in several rooms. He found a few files labeled "M" and stashed them into his duffel bag. He found a box full of newspaper clippings and police reports, referring to the numerous break-ins attributed to the Mongoose. Even though they could be easily collected by Lin's contacts, he thought that bringing them along would save some time and perhaps Spencer had made some notations in the margins.

There were numerous laptops, servers and CPUs scattered about the apartment—they were all in hibernation mode except for the small notebook attached to a comfortable looking La-Z-Boy chair by the *Mauka*[22] window. The other equipment in the apartment, though sophisticated looking, held no real promise of useful data.

He began to physically remove the hard drives from as many of the computers as possible. This was a relatively easy task. With expert hands and specialized tools, it took about sixty seconds per machine. After collecting ten hard drives, at least one from each work area in the apartment, he decided that he had enough hard data to keep Lin's analysts busy. He had not been gentle. Spencer would have to completely replace most of his computer systems.

He made himself comfortable in the La-Z-Boy chair and with a thumb drive he pulled from his vest pocket, he began the process of hacking through Spencer's ID and password protected firewall. This was taking longer than

---

[21] Digestive slumber, fall asleep after eating too much
[22] Mountain Side

expected, but once through, he knew that additional information could be found on Spencer's Cloud servers—if he could get through the 64-bit data encryption scheme in time.

He looked out the window and admired the view while he waited. A light mist hung over the valley.

"Nice place," he said.

His cell phone buzzed. Spencer's van had returned. *Time to go. Dammit...*

He hadn't gotten through the firewall, so he pulled the thumb drive and inserted another. It automatically downloaded the spyware code.

A minute later, he left the apartment and joined his colleagues on the 21st floor.

Chapter 19

As Maggie sorted through the treasures from the Dillingham house, deciding which items to keep and which to sell, she thought back to the events that began her transformation into her current life as the Mongoose. Her reflections naturally went to the Waimanalo farm.

When Mae-Linh Malia Nguyen Kawanakapili was released from prison in June 1993, she took refuge at the Kawanakapili *'Ohana*[23] Farm. She dropped her nickname, Maggie, and reverted to the Hawaiian name given by her parents, Malia. She adjusted easily to the rhythm of life on the farm.

She had been out of prison, the Women's Community Correctional Center (WCCC) for nearly a year before she returned to burglary as a profession. A four-year sentence for aggravated assault and drug possession had passed relatively quickly. In retrospect, life in prison had been the best thing for her. It had saved her life. Going cold turkey was no picnic, but she had been clean at that point for almost five years. Drugs had no power over her anymore. The control she now exerted over her emotions and life had come at great cost, but she was beginning to emerge from the great darkness that had surrounded her. Connecting with Mother Earth and her Hawaiian roots helped.

She placed a delicate ceramic statue of a ballerina into a box labeled Dillingham/Keep.

I was never that little girl.

She worked hard on her uncles' taro farm, but she was allowed frequent breaks from the toil and oppressive heat. On hot and humid summer afternoons, she enjoyed resting in the soft mist that rained down from the disappearing waterfalls

---

[23] Family

109

that originated three hundred feet above the valley floor. Tiny airborne droplets of moisture fell gently all around her, nourishing the orchids, bromeliads, and other jungle flowers clinging to the volcanic rock. Waterfalls of all kinds were very common along the Koolau Mountain range. When the rain was heavy, water fell uninterrupted a thousand feet to the bottom of the cliffs into clear pools, but when dry air circled the mountaintops, they became a trickle that turned into a fine cloud of moisture before reaching its destination. Malia preferred the mist—it matched her reflective mood.

The thirty-minute hike to her favorite waterfall was a ritual that her uncles and coworkers graciously granted her. They understood the feeling of freedom that Malia derived from spending some time wrapped in the serenity of the jungle, mountains and waterfalls of Waimanalo Valley. She appreciated their gift, and always worked doubly hard after her breaks.

As the soft mist caressed her exposed arms, legs and face, she had time to think about her time in prison and the dramatic turn her life had taken after dropping out of high school.

She had been lost, alone and depressed, barely keeping her head above water in the tragic swamp left by the death of her father, her brother, and the psychotic breakdown of her mother. The narcotics easily available in Chinatown gave her relief and temporarily filled the emptiness in her heart. Relatives and friends had tried to fill the void. They encouraged her to go back to school, to college or pursue a career, but she rejected them all and chose the life of a junkie. She disappeared into the underbelly of Honolulu.

Sitting in the cool, dry living room of her underground hideout, she now realized that life on the streets, the drugs, the petty theft and the dabbling in prostitution had made the hole more encompassing. The crack cocaine had mellowed her moods and brought some artificial happiness, but she'd felt most alive when jacked up on crystal meth. Honolulu belonged to her during those days—there was nothing she wouldn't try.

She had bounded through a series of abusive relationships and landed under the wing of a minor Chinatown gang boss. He saw the natural intelligence and promise of the girl, and taught her the art of drug dealing, burglary and the fencing of stolen goods. With his encouragement, Maggie slowly weaned herself off the harder drugs. She blossomed under his tutelage, but quickly crashed after his murder by a rival gang leader. The gaping hole turned into an abyss. She turned to the only relief she could find, more alcohol and drugs.

For several months, she wandered from Chinatown to Waikiki in a dazed state. She slept in the public parks or alleyways along River Street. The money she gained from prostitution, petty theft or begging, went to her addiction. She found meals at the River of life Mission—those do-gooders kept her body alive. Her mind was already gone.

Her most lucid moment during those years came on the last night before she was imprisoned. She had passed out along the Ala'wai Canal when the crystal meth had begun to wear off. She woke up to the sounds of two men raping her. One man held her down while the other pounded into her. They took turns.

At first, she thought she was dreaming. She didn't feel any pain, just an unusual numbness. She heard the Caucasian men talking casually about "enjoying a fuckin' freebie." They were taking their time. The moist grass on her lower back struck a nerve and suddenly she understood where she was, and where she had been for the last several years. The absolute horror of the situation penetrated the fog that blanketed her being. She grabbed a rock and smashed the man straddling her in the head. Blood splattered over her half-naked torso. She stood up, angry, viscous, ready to protect herself from the second man. He ran.

A few hours later, HPD arrested Maggie for aggravated assault and drug possession. The men, tourists from Australia, testified that she had attacked them without warning. The judge and jury believed the tourists over a homeless prostitute-junkie. The consensus was that Waikiki was safer, more tourist friendly, without people like her roaming the streets. Her court-appointed defense attorney claimed that the system had failed her client, Mae-Linh Malia Nguyen Kawanakapili. Maggie knew better, though, she had failed herself. She deserved life in prison.

I would have died in a dark dirty alley if not for that judge, she thought as she tossed a gold Rolex into the "For Sale" box.

Prison had been transforming for Maggie, and because of that, she was able to enjoy a peaceful life on the Waimanalo farm. It was a perfect place for her to slowly be re-introduced into society. There was a calm, predictable rhythm to the activities of the farm.

The extended Kawanakapili family, maybe thirty people on any given day, lived on the property and worked the successful enterprise. They sold local produce at the farmers markets in Kailua and Honolulu, and had contracts with Foodland and Times grocery stores for seasonal fruits and vegetables. Kawanakapili 'Ohana Farms *poi*,[24] sweet corn, watercress, butter lettuce, bananas, watermelon and papaya, were sought after throughout the island.

Soon after joining the farm community, she dropped her Caucasian nickname, and asked everyone to call her Malia, her given Hawaiian name. "Maggie" had served her

---

[24]Pounded Taro root

112

well in high school, during her crack and crystal meth years, and in prison, but that part of her life was gone. She intended to get in touch with her Hawaiian roots. This, she believed, is what her father and maybe her mother would have wanted.

Getting close to the land and learning the ways of the traditional native Hawaiian people had meaning and purpose—she was beginning to heal. The fine mist from the waterfall washed over her, cleansing the wounds of the past.

Maggie placed a polished Koa wood bowl and a delicate feather Lei on top of the other items in the "Keep" box, and breathed a sigh of satisfaction. She had finished sorting the Dillingham loot. There was enough to make a sizable donation to the Peanut Butter Ministry in Chinatown. They, like the family farm, had taken her in, when others had turned her away.

She remembered the day when she returned to the taro patch after a cool respite at the waterfall and she had been surprised to find that most of the adults were absent. She had asked one of the young boys, where everybody was.

"They go *'aha kū kā malū*[25] at the central house," he replied in half English, half Hawaiian.

"What's going on?" She asked in Hawaiian.

"I don't know. Everybody's upset, nothing good."

Malia ran to the central compound. She prayed that no one was hurt. She stopped short just as she entered the gathering place—a grassy area with picnic tables and a small earthen stage. All of the adults, about twenty people in all, were crowded around the stage listening to her great uncle, the patriarch of the Kawanakapili clan. A traditional discussion meeting was underway.

"Our appeal to The Office of Hawaiian Affairs has been reviewed with mixed results," he said in Hawaiian.

---

[25] A gathering to discuss

113

"Are we still threatened with eviction?" someone asked in English.

"No, that's the good news. OHA has ruled that as native Hawaiians, we have a right to live on this land. The courts agreed that the farm is part of the Royal Hawaiian ceded lands given to the Hawaiian people by our ancestors."

A cheer rose through the crowd.

Malia understood that the conflict with the other commercial farms on the Windward side of the island had been settled, at least for now. They had been trying for years to eliminate Kawanakapili farm. The native Hawaiian way of life, farming and commerce had proven to be stiff competition for the commercial farms—Monsanto, Dole, Castle and Cook. Kawanakapili produce grown organically, with family labor using methods that had been handed down through generations, was of better quality and could be sold more cheaply than products grown on the commercial farms.

Kawanakapili, by virtue of their native Hawaiian status, also had special tax provisions and protection that commercial farms did not have. The attorneys for the commercial farms tried to prove that the land was not actually Hawaiian ceded land, that it was private land given to the Kawanakapili family illegally by the last Hawaiian King, David Kalākaua. Their goal was to close the farm and parcel up the land between them.

"The bad news?" someone asked. A silent hush fell over the crowd.

"OHA has declared our family claim to the land—void," the last word he said in English. Malia wasn't sure if it was for emphasis, or perhaps there was no comparable word in the Hawaiian language.

He gestured, sweeping his muscular arms towards the ocean. "They say the land belongs to all of the Hawaiian people," the patriarch said. "They wish to build a Hawaiian Homelands subdivision on our property."

There were murmurs of confusion throughout the crowd.

"All the lands belong to the Hawaiian people," someone said. "That's true."

"We are Hawaiian. Our family is descended from generations that have lived and farmed these very lands for thousands of years," another said.

"OHA is a government agency. They have no right to control the sovereignty of our Hawaiian nation. These lands belong to us," someone else shouted.

The patriarch looked at the crowd and shook his head slowly. He waited until the crowd quieted.

"As always, the situation is complicated and difficult to understand. In some way, I think we can all understand OHA's position. We have no legal documents that give us claim to this land we call Kawanakapili farm. We only have the oral traditions of five generations and the notations in the King's accounts. As a native people, we agree that the land belongs to everyone. Before modern times, only the *Ali'i*[26] controlled the land for the good of the people. OHA now sees itself in that position."

"What can be done?"

"I am told that if we allow one third of our lands closest to the shoreline to be used as a subdivision, the rest of our farm can be purchased for a reasonable sum."

"That's thievery!" someone exclaimed. "Buy our own land."

"Our rights as Hawaiians are being stripped," another said.

"It's extortion!"

---

[26] Hawaiian Royalty

Malia's uncle held his hands over his head and asked his family to be patient.

"We will consider this offer," he said. "It may be the only way to secure the land for future generations."

"But, even if we did accept their terms, do we have enough money to purchase our own land?"

"It is a very large sum that they are asking," he answered. "The elders will be busy over the next few weeks considering this offer and determining if we can somehow raise the money required. Focus on your families and our farm for now. We have won a great battle, and we should be grateful for that measure of success."

Malia listened carefully. Her Hawaiian language skills were limited but she understood most of what the leader of the clan had said.

Over the next few weeks as discussions over the offer went on, it became clear that the elders wanted to make a deal with OHA. The huge amount of money would have to be raised through donations, fundraisers and bank loans. Everyone would have to pitch-in and tighten their belts.

It was during this time, that Malia decided that she would use the skills she had developed living on the streets of Chinatown and in prison to help her family. It was a difficult decision, but these aunts and uncles, nephews and nieces were her 'ohana. They had welcomed her and had saved her from a life of drugs and crime. She realized that they would not be able to raise the money in time. She believed she was the only one who could do it. She owed them everything.

It was the right thing to do.

She remembered coming to that conclusion quite easily. She still felt the same way, but now, after all of these years, something felt different.

She had contacted a few trustworthy acquaintances from her prison days that were still connected to the Honolulu underworld to help her. She practiced in the early morning hours, planned carefully, and honed her skills.

To justify her actions, she developed a code. She would only take cash, jewelry and valuable artifacts from the most wealthy and powerful landowners in the state. She would be selective and target the family or business purposely. All of her profits would go to help her people. She promised herself that this would be a temporary lapse back into crime. As soon as the farm was secure, she would stop.

She had committed three major burglaries over the next six months and anonymously donated large amounts of cash to the Kawanakapili Farm coffers. The farm was saved, purchased legally and forever from the Department of Hawaiian Homelands. The Waimanalo subdivision was eventually built and hundreds of native Hawaiian families were given the opportunity to have their own homes.

Malia had been successful, but she soon learned that her unique brand of altruism was also a drug, almost as addictive as crystal meth. She told herself she would do it just one more time—over and over again.

The planning, the preparation and the execution of the burglaries filled her with energy and purpose she had never felt before. After each successful hit, the physical and emotional satisfaction grew, until it consumed her. Punishing those that would steal from her people was orgasmic. She was hooked. She found countless reasons to continue her newfound profession.

A year later, she left the farm and moved into the ammunition bunkers in Waikele.

She ordered her men to call her Maggie.

I left Malia and my ohana behind, she thought as she stacked the "Keep" box on a shelf in one of the back tunnels.

Chapter 20

They returned from the hospital to find that the penthouse was a complete wreck—books, files, documents, computer parts and wires had been trashed and scattered about, littering the once tidy apartment. Lillian broke down in tears when she saw how the place had been ransacked. Pablo immediately started to clean up and put some things back in order. James sat quietly in his wheelchair and waited for his caregiver to compose herself. He understood that the apartment was just as much her home as it was his.

When the initial shock wore off, James had Pablo take him through every room and corner of the penthouse. He took a mental inventory of the damage. Clearly, someone was looking for information. What that was, he had no idea.

It would take several hours of careful study to determine if there was a pattern to the chaotic mess, a thread indicating what data had been targeted. Replacing the computer equipment would be no problem. Rebuilding the system configurations would take a little bit of time, but everything was automatically backed-up on his own private cloud servers. Lillian would be able to reassemble, the furniture, the files, books and documents. The attack was more of a nuisance than anything else.

He called Detective Morimoto, told him what happened and asked that a couple of crime scene investigators be sent over. He doubted seriously that they would find anything useful, but at least he would have a complete record of the damage for insurance purposes.

When pressed by the detective, James answered honestly that he really had no idea who had ransacked his place. However, he did note to the detective that it seemed to be a professional job and the motivation seemed to point towards the gathering of specific information.

When Morimoto suggested that the break-in might have had something to do with Lou's kidnapping, James agreed that there was a possible connection, but withheld what he suspected about the identity of the Mongoose and the threatening messages he had received. The detective pressed further, sensing that Spencer was holding something back.

James heard the skepticism in Morimoto's voice and the doubt in his probing questions. He answered superficially, but that was as far as he was willing to go with the detective. He was convinced Maggie had nothing to gain by attacking his home. Her message had already been received loud and clear. There were no additional messages left behind or any signs that *she* had visited his apartment.

The damage was surgical—confined to computers and files, not driven by theft, revenge or random vandalism, the Mongoose's usual mode of operation. Someone was looking for something. James felt sure that if Maggie was involved, it was indirectly. The conversation with Morimoto ended unsatisfactorily for both of them.

"Mister Spencer, you need to take your medication. Then rest for while," Lillian said after he'd made an initial sweep of the apartment. She was still visibly upset, and needed to rest herself.

"Lillian, let Pablo take care of me for while. You get some rest."

She reluctantly retreated to her bedroom. Pablo was perfectly willing to help-out for as long as needed. After a bowl of hot soup and some medication, James settled into his bed and began to examine the Notebook that was usually attached to the La-Z-Boy by the Pali Highway window.

This was the only computer in the penthouse that had been left powered-on—a mistake that he instantly regretted.

All of the other equipment had been shut-down and secured, that's why the perpetrator had no other choice but to physically remove the hard drives in order to get the information he or she was after. This Notebook, because it had been left on, was vulnerable and had no doubt been a source of intense interest.

As he scanned the computer and ran various diagnostics, he replayed the final few minutes of his meeting with Lou in his head.

The hospital room had felt unusually cool and sterile. Lou had been visibly upset.

"What do you mean it's Maggie?" Lou had asked.

"She's the one behind your kidnapping, the IEDs..."

"You're crazy. Neither of us has had any contact with her for over twenty years. What possible reason could she have for wanting to harm us?" Lou said." I mean...me."

"You're right when you say us. Hurting you was a way to get me as well."

"This can't be about Luke. That was too long ago."

James had paused and thought carefully before making his next utterance.

"Maggie is the Mongoose."

Lou looked at James with shock and confusion written across his face.

"You better explain yourself."

James knew that Maggie was Lou's first love, and that even though that was thirty years past, and he had had many relationships since, Lou might still be emotionally raw over the rejection he had suffered so long ago. Without the implants to assist with the balancing of his brain processes, James was aware that his friend's memories, emotions, cognition, physical and chemical responses might be impaired or overly reactive.

Reliving his time with Maggie could trigger additional tragic memories from his tours of duty in Lebanon, Iraq and Afghanistan. This could complicate his already severe PTSD symptoms or adversely affect sites within his brain that had suffered TBI. James needed to tread lightly.

"Just the facts. You draw your own conclusions," James said. "Remember several years back when the HPD and FBI gave up on the Mongoose case."

He forced himself to breathe.

"All of their leads had grown stone cold. Something about the MO bothered me and when my family home in Manoa was hit, I began to investigate."

"I remember you mentioning it. Not a top priority for us as we held no real sympathy for the wealthy and powerful targets."

"Exactly, I think that's what bothered me," James said. "Anyway, I began to collect everything I could about the targets and the so-called Mongoose. I kept my involvement under the radar, not wanting any pressure or interference from the HPD."

"And...the facts, please."

"The thefts were understandable; the strange part was the vandalism. The Mongoose was sending a message. The need to punish and inflict personal damage was very clear. These were more than just robberies."

"Revenge?" Lou asked.

James nodded slightly, and continued. "Then I noticed a strange pattern of large cash donations made to small nonprofit charities throughout the islands—each within a couple of weeks after the robberies."

"Classic Robin Hood, how quaint..."

"Yes, quite altruistic. Most charities were native Hawaiian associated."

"A radicalized Hawaiian activist?" Lou adjusted himself in the hospital bed. "Sounds like a good cause to me, but I still don't see the connection to Maggie."

"You joined the Marines and understandably lost touch with her," James continued. "I however, came home during summer breaks and Christmas vacations. I never stopped trying to connect with Maggie. On a couple of occasions, I did manage to track her down."

"You bastard, you never told me that."

James flinched, as much as his frozen body would allow.

"Lou, you would not have recognized her. Her spiral into depression led to drug addiction, and finally jail time. She didn't want anything to do with me, or you."

Sounding more like a doctor than a friend James continued. "She went through a lot. Prison. Cold turkey withdrawal. She had been raped... I represented deep pain, loss and tragedy—a past she wanted to forget. She screamed at me when I visited her at WCCC."

Lou's face softened.

"After she got out, she went to live on her uncle's farm on Hawaiian lands in Waimanalo. I lost track of her after that."

"So you think she may have been radicalized by them?"

"It's possible, but not really that probable. The Hawaiian sovereignty groups her Uncles belonged to were politically radical, but most did not condone any violence or direct social unrest."

"So something else must have set her off," Lou said.

"That's when I began to investigate her father's death more closely. It turns out his death in the construction accident was caused by severe negligence...Negligence by the contractors."

James' voice got softer, not because of the information he was sharing, but because of his lack of air and energy. Lou leaned closer.

"If you remember, when the building collapsed, six men lost their lives. There was an inquiry and some accusations, but the developers behind the scene squashed the investigation. There was a major cover-up involving several powerful local families, state investigators and city government. The police and possibly one or two judges may have also been involved—it was a huge mess."

"Holy shit, how did you figure all this out?"

"You don't really want me to go into all the details, do you?"

"Nope, just always amazed at your ability to put things together."

"Thanks Lou."

"Don't expect any other compliments. Just continue with your story."

"So the families were paid off. The lawsuits were dropped. The downtown building was built and sold for a very handsome profit."

"And so you believe that it's a combination of factors that made Maggie become the infamous Mongoose."

"Well, yeah. Also, there's some other weird stuff."

Lou waited until James caught his breath.

"Soon after I came to the realization that it might be Maggie, bouquets of tropical flowers began to be delivered anonymously to my apartment on a regular basis—a bunch arrived the day you were kidnapped. They always include Ginger. Then, I began having reoccurring dreams, or nightmares, from that day at Jackass Pool."

"Okay, now you're freaking me out. While I was tied up in that basement, I almost got sick from the smell of the Ginger," Lou said. "I had a weird and very vivid recollection of Luke's death, among other things, while lying on that cold floor."

James was tired. It was the most conversation he'd had in a long time.

Lou looked tired too.

"Last thing... While you were being held, a photograph with an encrypted message came to me. It was a warning to back off working cold cases with the HPD. The photograph was of all of us at Tantalus. I suspect it was taken by Luke."

James deliberately left out the fact that he had received several similar encrypted messages over the last couple of years. There was no need to upset the apple cart any further.

"What do you mean all of us?"

"You, me, Maggie, Johnny and Shingo."

That had been enough for James to connect the dots, and from the sudden slouch of Lou's shoulders and the tired expression on his face, James could tell there was enough evidence for Lou as well.

They talked about a few more things, and pondered how Maggie had gone so far astray. They both inwardly wondered if there was something more they could have done, they should have done. James left the hospital relieved, but exhausted.

He had slept on the ride home.

Beep beep beep, his Notebook called.

The virus scanner had completed its job. He read through the report. The usual Internet Spam and cyber hack jobs had been detected. He saw nothing out of the ordinary, except for one unusual piece of Spyware. He had found no evidence that the perpetrator had been able to penetrate his firewall, but the Spyware was interesting. It might have been loaded onto the Notebook manually.

James isolated the code. He would dissect it later. Perhaps it would lead to the careful professional that had violated his home.

He called his IT team and began the process of rebuilding.

Chapter 21

Jefferson Hammerhead's technology guys were not the best that money could buy, but they did a fairly adequate job. They had come up with a few interesting pieces of information about the Mongoose after plowing through the hard drives and documents retrieved from Doctor Spencer's apartment.

It was clear that James Spencer knew much more about the thief than he was telling the HPD. If the Spyware his man had planted continued to function, Jefferson felt he would have a good lead to follow soon enough—something that would take him directly to the Mongoose. It was time to pay a personal visit to Mr. Lin. He always found that the personal touch worked more effectively, especially when more money was required and questions needed to be answered.

As Jefferson rode the elevator to the 46th floor of the Bishop Towers building, he consciously pumped himself up, straightened his posture and made sure his three-piece suit was lint and wrinkle free. He wiped the sweat from his brow with a silk handkerchief. The walk from Chinatown had been hot and humid. He preferred slacks and an Aloha shirt, but this was a special occasion. It was not every day that he had business downtown where tie-adorned attorneys, accountants and CEOs wandered the sidewalks and alleyways.

The Hammerhead had decided to ask for $50,000 additional payment for his services. He had no idea why this Mongoose was so important to Chinn Ho Lin, but he suspected that Lin was just a go-between. His actual employers no doubt had very deep pockets and his reputation required that he take advantage of the situation. He certainly didn't want powerbrokers on the island to think his services came cheap or without obligation.

"Mister Chinn Ho Lin, please," Jefferson said politely.

"Do you have an appointment?" the receptionist asked without looking up from her computer screen.

"Eye contact is polite and required, young lady," Jefferson said. Then a little more firmly, "I don't have an appointment, and you will let Mister Lin know that I'm here. My name is Michael Jefferson."

The receptionist looked up and saw a six-foot-five giant of a man looming over the front of her desk. His voice was polite and educated. She guessed from his accent that he was from New Zealand or Australia. He had a broad smile and bright white teeth that contrasted with his dark Polynesian skin. His smile and mannerisms were friendly, but they also sent the message that he meant business and was not to be taken lightly.

"Yes, sir. Please have a seat. I will inform Mister Lin that you are here."

"That won't be necessary my dear. Just point me to Mister Lin's office and I will see myself in," Jefferson said. "And please don't touch that security alarm under your desk. It's totally unnecessary I can assure you."

He opened his vest just enough to reveal the black handle of his pistol.

The receptionist, now wide-eyed and shaking, pointed down the hall.

"Thank you."

Jefferson strode purposefully to the large corner office, opened the door and let himself in. Chinn Ho Lin was busy talking on the phone and shuffling papers.

"I'll call you later," he said looking up from his desk. "What the hell are you doing here?"

"I thought I'd pay a visit, but before we get too cozy please let your lovely receptionist know that I'm a welcome guest and there's no need for alarm."

Lin made the call, while Jefferson made himself comfortable in a big leather chair just in front of the realtor's huge mahogany desk. The spacious office and the large desk made the tiny Chinese businessman seem even smaller than he actually was. His balding head reflected the light coming from the tinted windows. His pudgy stomach bumped against the side of the desk. Jefferson had met his current employer on a couple of occasions and was always amazed at how nervous and fidgety the man was. They were complete opposites—Lin was clearly uncomfortable in his skin and perpetually anxious, while the Hammerhead oozed physical confidence and inner serenity.

"What do you want?"

"I have some new information to share with you, if you're so inclined," Jefferson said.

"Why not just send it to me?"

"Too much trouble, I'd have to dictate a letter and have it delivered. It's much more enjoyable to take a stroll downtown. You know my office is just ten minutes walk from here. You should really come visit me sometime."

"Get out with it," Lin said, arranging papers and knickknacks on his desk.

"Spencer knows who the Mongoose is."

"Really, who is he?"

"It's a she."

"Fascinating, tell me more," Lin said, finally leaning back in his chair, almost relaxing.

"The Mongoose is a local girl that goes by the name Mae-Linh Malia Nguyen Kawanakapili."

"Vietnamese – Hawaiian?"

"Yes, born in Honolulu. Vietnamese mother and a Hawaiian father. Her father died while she was in high school. A tragic construction accident, you might remember."

"What do you mean?"

"I mean, we all have our secrets. The fact that you profited greatly from the building where your lovely office is located, and that you and a few others orchestrated the cover-up of the collapse of Bishop Towers, is safe with me."

"I see you're quite thorough," Lin said, not surprised that the Hammerhead knew this tidbit of information. "But this isn't about me. Tell me more about the girl. Where is she?"

"Her brother died in a swimming accident a couple of years later. Her mother went psycho soon after and has been in and out of treatment for years. The girl spent a few years in my part of town, enjoying the pleasures we have to offer and learning the tricks of the trade—prostitution, burglary, petty theft, drug addiction. She served four years at WCCC."

Lin leaned forward in his chair. His fidgety demeanor returned.

"Last known address Kawanakapili Farms in Waimanalo," Jefferson said, reaching over and stopping Lin's nervous tapping. "That's all I have at the moment."

"Have you checked out the farm?" Lin asked, pulling his arm away.

"She hasn't been seen there for over twelve years. She's off the grid. It's going to take more money and more time to find her."

"How much more?"

"$50,000 and two or three weeks."

Jefferson pulled out a packet of information from his vest pocket and placed it on Lin's desk.

"This is some of the raw evidence to show your pals," Jefferson said as he stood up and towered over the still seated little man.

"I'll send one of my boys over tomorrow afternoon to pick up the cash."

"But... I have to check with," Lin stammered.

"With whom?" Jefferson replied quickly. "I'd be happy to go directly to them."

"Okay, okay."

"Good. Then have a nice day Mister Chinn Ho Lin."

Chapter 22

Lou sat in the Starbucks on Bishop Street across the street from the Aloha Internet Café. He sipped his ice-coffee and scanned each person going in and out of the Internet Café. He was on stakeout following a lead James had discovered after hours of analysis and cyber-sifting.

He had tracked the origin of the photograph with the warning message. It had traveled around the world, through cyberspace, and somehow to this particular hole in the wall on Bishop Street. How his partner had managed to come up with a face and a name, Lou would never understand, but it hadn't surprised him—he understood that James' mental faculties compensated for his physical limitations.

Yin and Yang.

Lou hated being on stakeout. The music in the Starbucks irritated him.

"Hey, Jimmy," Lou said. "How about piping in some decent music?"

"Okay, I've got some new indie tunes for you. Just recorded from the South by Southwest festival."

James, the voice in his head, came through loud and clear. The surgery had been successful and they both thought the upgrades to the implants were a big improvement. The clarity of reception on both sides was exceptional and the few new functions that James had included would no doubt prove to be very useful.

"Great, anything would be better than this New Age Jazz they're playing."

"Enjoy," James said.

Lou detected a hint of happiness in James' voice. Things had been going very well the last few weeks. He had recovered completely and their friendship was stronger than ever. Lou thought that James especially enjoyed it when he had started to call him "Jimmy" rather than James—which he did more often than not these days. It reminded them both of their long-standing friendship.

"What about that grungy looking dude?" Lou asked.

"Nope, but he does have three outstanding parking tickets."

James was running advanced facial recognition software in the background. Every face that Lou focused on was immediately analyzed using several public, private and government databases. The artificial intelligence (AI) software stripped down each face to its base elements and literally searched the world for a match.

It was probably overkill, they had the guy's picture already, but James liked to run the new software through its paces. Each time they ran a real scenario the AI got better and faster. Lou thought it was amusing to be able to find out all sorts of public and private information about a person just by looking into their face.

Privacy was a thing of the past.

"Tell me about that good-looking Korean chick," Lou said.

"Just a minute, pervert."

"You enjoy this just as much as I do," Lou laughed. "You're just jealous that I can act on my impulses."

"She's Chinese, not Korean. She's out of your league, married with children."

"You're right, I'm looking for a dancer or a waitress," Lou said as he continued to scan the street and the entrance to the Internet Café.

"Here's something interesting," James said. "Michael Hammerhead Jefferson, just coming out of Bishop Tower."

Lou's eyes followed the known mobster as he sauntered down the street towards Chinatown.

"Not our guy, or our business. But, sure interesting that he was visiting someone in this part of town," James said.

"All dressed up too."

Lou turned his attention back to the Internet café.

Suddenly, the sounds of semi-automatic gunfire broke the peaceful din of downtown traffic, piped in New Age Jazz and business conversations. Lou hit the deck and instinctively drew his Glock. He heard screams, cars screeching and fenders bending, but no broken glass or bullets in the Starbucks.

"What the fuck?"

"Lou, are you okay?" The voice inside his head said.

Without answering, Lou holstered his gun and ran down the street. He pushed his way through a crowd on the corner of Bishop and King. The impeccably dressed Hammerhead lay dead in a pool of dark red blood.

Chapter 23

Maggie heard the gunshots from inside the Aloha Internet Café. Her first reaction was to ditch the meeting with her key IT geek and get away from downtown as quickly as possible. She could slip out the back exit where her driver was waiting, and be safely down the H1 in less than five minutes. However, after taking a breath she realized that she was incognito and no one was looking for her. Only James Spencer and perhaps Jefferson, the Hammerhead—now that his men had hit Spencer's apartment—had any clue that she was the Mongoose, or that she even existed.

She sipped her sweet tea and continued her conversation with her companion. The geek and the Mongoose made a strange pair, but this was a dark and dingy café and no one had looked twice at the odd couple. Now with all of the commotion outside, there was not even a slim chance that someone was paying attention to them.

The geek sitting across from her was a greasy black haired Asian man, much younger and much less refined. His pock marked face looked like it hadn't seen soap for ages. She reminded him of a freshly pan-fried pot-sticker—crispy brown around the edges, with a soft, odorous pale gray flesh inside. He was disheveled, dirty, and looked borderline homeless, while she was his polar opposite—immaculately dressed, clean, trim and proper.

The Mongoose was assuming her public persona, a 40-year-old blonde, blue-eyed caucasian named Mary Jay Higgins.

Mary had been painstakingly fabricated in 1995, a year after Maggie had left the farm. When Mary began to make her physical and digital presence known to the world, Mae-Linh Malia Nguyen Kawanakapili—Maggie, had quietly disappeared. For the last twenty years, she never went out in public without Mary Jay. She was a very useful part of her existence—allowing her to interact with the rest of the world without fear of being discovered. Mary Jay had even befriended her mother, so that Mae-Linh could visit and keep tabs on her treatment and well-being.

Mary Jay finished her business with the geek, foregoing any further small talk. She requested another message be sent to Spencer over the Internet, this time using a photograph from Jackass Ginger Pool. She slipped the man an envelope with the photograph, the text for the message, and enough cash to keep him happy for a while. She figured he would blow half of it on computer equipment—geeks always needed faster and newer machines. She flinched when their hands touched and some of her powdered white makeup rubbed off on his greasy fingers.

Clumsy twit, she said to herself, referring to both of them.

I have to be more careful.

She stood up from the table, dismissed the geek who was eager to be off to the nearest Best Buy, and walked as steadily as possible on her four-inch lift shoes to the bathroom at the back of the café. She washed her hands and looked at herself in the mirror. Everything was still in place. She adjusted her short blonde wig and the bodysuit that made her look thirty pounds heavier. She made sure her one-piece dress and demure accessories were in place, and then indulging her curiosity, she left the café and merged with the gawkers on street.

It had been a long time since there had been a shooting in downtown Honolulu in the middle of the day. The media and smart phone wielding public were sensationalizing the events within minutes, long before HPD managed to take control of the situation.

One poor woman had even been pushed into the pool of blood flowing from the crosswalk into a nearby storm drain. She sat on the bus stop bench hyperventilating, still traumatized from getting blood splattered on her high heels and bare legs. A Honolulu Star-Advertiser photographer was gently posing her, taking shots from numerous angles. Undoubtedly, one would show up on tomorrow morning's front page.

Maggie was surprised to see Lou Costelilia helping the rookie cops control the growing throng of people. She knew he was in town, but Bishop Street was a long way from the governor's office or Spencer's place. This was not his neighborhood, but the fact that he was helping-out didn't faze her. He had always been a first responder—the first to help someone in danger, the first to climb the Stairway to Heaven, the first to try the rope swing at Jackass Ginger, the first to jump in to save her brother.

What is he doing here?

She took one look at the dead body lying face up in the road and then faded back into the crowd. She was shocked to see that the dead man was Michael Kalani Jefferson, the notorious Chinatown gang leader known as the "Hammerhead." She recognized him immediately, even though he wasn't wearing his usual Aloha shirt and khaki pants.

Ironic, she thought. *Looks like he was dressed for a funeral... His own.*

Blood was everywhere. He must have been shot at least six times. Strangely, though, his face was clean and unblemished.

Maggie remembered the face very well. He was one of the few gangsters in Chinatown that had shown her any respect. Jefferson, before he was known as the "Hammerhead," had been a lieutenant for one of the up-and-coming mixed race gangs. He had suggested that she give up drugs and prostitution, and work for him as a full-time burglar. He recognized her skills. He had introduced her to a professional Burglar that eventually became her mentor. She recalled what Jefferson had told her.

"It takes more than physical strength and moxy to make a good thief. You need patience, intelligence and stealth. A quiet hit and clean getaway are always preferable to a noisy and messy job."

In the short time that she knew him, Maggie had learned quite a bit from Jefferson and she still followed his advice today. Her entrances and exits were well planned, quiet and flawless, though she doubted he would approve of her fondness for vandalism—too messy. She felt a slight tinge of sadness to know that he was dead—perhaps it was just nostalgia, a yearning for youth and possibilities.

The EMS arrived and the police presence increased exponentially. Traffic was stalled, and it was clear that the downtown area would be bottled up for quite a while. She watched for a couple more minutes and then made her way to the alley behind Bishop Towers where her driver was waiting.

I wonder who had Jefferson killed? She asked herself as the car sped west out of Honolulu.

I guess it doesn't matter, he was getting too close. Someone saved me from having to deal with him.

The Mongoose didn't have the sophisticated surveillance and analytical technology of James Spencer, but she had physical eyes and ears throughout the city. She knew about the Big-Five families and their contract out on her head. She knew about Chinn Ho Lin's involvement and the break-in to Spencer's apartment orchestrated by Jefferson.

She cautiously assumed that they had gathered enough information by now to threaten her existence. The question was how much had the Hammerhead revealed to Lin before he was gunned down.

She guessed that Jefferson had probably just finished visiting Lin's office. It was strange that he had gotten all dressed-up and visited the powerful realtor personally.

Why not just communicate by phone or a go-between? There must've been something important he wanted to deliver, or an angle that he was playing.

The car slowed at the H1 – H2 merge.

Whatever it was, he was gone now.

Maggie watched the traffic slip by.

Too many damn cars.

Chapter 24

James stayed busy scanning the crowd and collecting as much data as possible while Lou did his thing—crowd control, schmoozing with the first responders, consoling some stupid woman who had stepped in the victim's blood, and talking to detective Morimoto. The detective had arrived on the scene almost immediately. A little too quickly, James thought, but then again, a shooting in downtown Honolulu was just the type of front-page exposure Morimoto sought.

Lou, on the other hand, avoided the limelight and preferred to dispense his brand of justice with as little fanfare as possible. He was more comfortable behind the scenes, doing the grunt work. He didn't need recognition.

James felt as if Lou enjoyed police work too much. He realized however that it was just his friend's leadership skills and genuine compassion for others kicking in. He'd always been a leader, a first responder, a risk taker and an addict to altruism. He led by example. These characteristics had made him a great Marine, and a better friend. However, the contrast between Lou's ability to commit horrendously violent acts during wartime or in the name of justice, and his need to care for and lead others was an enigma. James struggled to understand it.

"Lou, give the crowd one more sweep."

Lou complied and tried to make eye contact with as many people as possible. They both knew that contract killers often hung around afterwards, or they paid someone to watch the scene while the police collected evidence. Criminals often employed this precaution because there was much to be learned from the movements of the detectives and crime scene investigators. This information was often the difference between imprisonment and freedom.

James was grateful that Lou didn't dwell on the body. He felt responsible for Jefferson's death—no remorse, just a strange, probably misplaced sense of responsibility. He knew he had not pulled the trigger or ordered the kill, but the actions he had taken over the last couple of weeks incriminating Jefferson of embezzling money from his own organization had more than likely resulted in the murder. James had hoped to distract Jefferson, not eliminate him. He certainly had not imagined that the mobster would be gunned down in the middle of Honolulu. He felt queasy.

"Lillian," he said into the intercom. "Can you bring me something for my stomach?"

"Get your own damn warm milk," Lou replied.

"Oh, sorry," James answered. He had forgotten to switch his connection with Lou to mute.

"Right away, Mister Spencer," Lillian replied.

Determining that Jefferson was behind the break-in of his apartment had been easy. Closed-circuit video from the security cameras for his condominium had pinpointed the three Akamai Air Conditioner installers as his prime suspects. They all had connections to the Hammerhead organization. The Spyware they had left behind had also proven to be useful, he kept it isolated but well fed with bogus information that the Chinatown boss might find interesting. A couple of times he watched as Jefferson and his operatives acted on information he had supplied to them. He had taken great pleasure in wasting the crime boss' time.

Jefferson's connection with Chinn Ho Lin had been a surprise, but the fact that the Big-Five families had put a contract out for the Mongoose, though disturbing, was expected. They'd had enough. Working through Lin and Jefferson, they were taking matters into their own hands.

The information Jefferson's men had taken from his apartment, if analyzed efficiently could lead to her identity.

From there, the combined resources of the Hammerhead organization and the Big-Five families would eventually be able to pin point her location. That was something he could never allow, he had to get to her first.

With Jefferson out of the picture, Maggie's chances of escaping detection had grown considerably. He was grateful for that, and yet he felt as if he may have played a major role in someone's death—a cold-blooded murder. Lou would congratulate him on a job well done. He would understand his actions and agree with the outcomes, but James was a virgin to this kind of violence. He had never purposely let anything die, except for perhaps a few lab rats or dissected rabbits during his medical training. This series of events would haunt him for a long time.

"Here you go, Mister Spencer," Lillian said proffering a straw connected to a mug of hot chocolate.

"Perfect, thank you Lillian."

James switched off the video and audio link with Lou. The recordings continued.

I will check them out later after resting.

Chapter 25

Detective Morimoto arrived on the scene irritated and exhausted as usual. The traffic was so badly bottlenecked at the Bishop and King intersection that he had to park his cruiser on the curb a hundred yards from where the body was located.

"Get these people out of here," he yelled at the closest police officers. "And for Christ sake, get the traffic moving!"

Morimoto was a small, slender man, but he had a big voice and a large reputation. He was always grumpy and treated everyone with disdain. He hated rookie cops for their innocence, energy and stupidity. He disliked the veteran officers just as much, feeling that they were generally lazy and dulled by years of paper pushing.

He could've easily made "Chief" years ago, but his gruff personality and outspoken stance on the police bureaucracy kept him out of the running. That didn't bother Morimoto, his true love was being in the field on the crime scene—there he was in charge and he garnered the recognition he deserved. Working behind the desk and supervising others would have killed him.

He pushed his way through the crowd surrounding the victim.

"It's Michael Kalani Jefferson, a.k.a. Hammerhead," the CSI lead said to him. "It looks like a professional hit, six shots to the torso."

"No shit Sherlock, want to just have your boys stand back for a few minutes while I take a look."

"As you wish," the CSI replied.

"Ass-wipe," Morimoto said under his breath, but just loud enough for everyone to hear.

He lit his electronic cigarette and took a deep drag. Quitting tobacco had helped his blood pressure, but soured his mood considerably. The great white clouds of water vapor were satisfying and the amount of nicotine he consumed was adequate, but without the heaviness of tar and the other chemicals found in regular cigarettes, the smoke just didn't fill his lungs enough. He wondered if he could inject something other than nicotine into the liquid cartridges to take the edge off, maybe cocaine.

He recognized Jefferson immediately. He looked unusually calm and comfortable dressed in his best three-piece suit, but he looked out of place. This gang leader rarely left Chinatown, and the only other time Morimoto had seen him dressed in a suit was in court or at a funeral. No doubt, he had come downtown on some special business.

"I want all the closed-circuit video footage from a three block radius," Morimoto told the supervising sergeant. "Jefferson was here on business. I want to know where he visited and who."

A professional had certainly targeted him. All six shots had hit the torso. Morimoto groaned. The last thing he needed was a professional hit man roaming the streets. It was bad enough that this was probably a gang related execution.

"How many shots were fired?"

"Six that we know of, Sir," one of the CSI's replied, immediately regretting his answer.

Morimoto just stared at him in disbelief.

"I'll have some of the officers canvas the witnesses and find out for you ASAP," the CSI said quickly.

"Hell'uv an idea."

Jefferson had no packages or any interesting evidence on his body. The only thing Morimoto found was an unusually fat money clip. He gave it to one of the CSI's to bag. He decided there was nothing else he could learn from the scene. He would have to wait for the video surveillance and officers' interviews to learn more. He left the scene and took a seat on the bench across the street in Bishop Square.

"Who wanted Jefferson killed?" He said to himself.

"Almost everyone," he answered. *"But gangland execution style, in the middle of downtown..."* Morimoto had a habit of carrying on a conversation with himself, especially when he was feeling stressed.

"Strange as there have been no rumors of turf wars between the gangs."

"Perhaps it was just someone attempting to move up in the organization."

"Yeah, and maybe it will snow in the Koolau's tonight," Morimoto chuckled. He was even sarcastic with himself. He enjoyed his own witty humor. He spotted Lou Costelilia helping the rookie cops with crowd control.

"Hey Costelilia!" He shouted. "Let the rookies do that. Get your ass over here!"

Lou recognized Morimoto's voice. He obediently trotted across the street and sat down next to the detective.

"What the hell are you doing here?

"Just in the neighborhood running an errand, thought I'd lend a hand," Lou said.

"I don't suppose you would like to tell me what that errand might be, and what it has to do with the mobster lying dead in the street," Morimoto said.

"Nope, and nothing. Just happened to be in the Starbucks enjoying my coffee when shots were fired."

"How many?"

"I counted six."

"Semi-automatic?"

"Sounded like a Bushmaster."

"Professional job?"

"That's your *kuliana*[27] detective," Lou said. "But six shots fired—six shots on target. No collateral damage."

"How you feeling by the way?"

"Never better. Thanks again to you and your officers for finding me," he touched the back of his head unconsciously. "Grant and Suzuki doing okay?"

"Both back on the job."

"Spencer sends his regards," Lou said.

"Sure, tell him I'd like Black Label for Christmas."

"Will do."

Both men sat quietly on the bench watching the traffic crawl by. Lou twiddled his thumbs waiting for Morimoto to get to the point. The detective relished his water vapor cigarette, in no hurry.

"Costelilia, don't you think it's strange that the IEDs were configured to cause injury and not kill?"

"Yeah, that is weird. But no clue as to what it means and still no idea who was behind my abduction."

"Really? It's hard to believe Spencer hasn't figured this out yet," Morimoto said, giving him a dissatisfied look.

"Facts are facts, got to get on with life. You ought to try that yourself."

"Work life balance, sure I hear that all the time," Morimoto said taking an extra long drag on his water vapor's cigarette.

Just not that satisfying, he thought.

"Anyway, you ever get tired of babysitting Spencer and working for the Governor, come see me," Morimoto said as he stood up from the bench. The Sergeant in charge was calling to him.

"I just might, someday. Have a good day detective."

"You too, Costelilia."

---

[27] Your area of expertise, responsibility

Morimoto joined his colleagues, asking questions and giving directions. He suspected that Costelilia and Spencer knew a lot more than they were sharing. If things weren't so busy all the time, he would delve a little deeper into the daily activities of the pair. For now, there was too much other BS to take care of.

Chapter 26

It started to rain in the early evening. Not the typical Tradewind showers that lasted just a few minutes as they blew over the islands, but a heavy humid downpour brought by light winds from the south. A low front had moved in, promising flash floods and possible thunderstorms.

The rain didn't bother the patrons of the Pacific Club. Their chauffeur driven sedans dropped them off under the front canopy and they made their way safely in to the air-conditioned inner sanctuary of the club. Jonathan Ward and Walter Kobayashi arrived early as planned. They met privately in a small lounge at the very back of the property.

"Look, John, I didn't expect it to happen in the middle of the day, a block from my offices," Walter Kobayashi said, cleaning his wire-rimmed glasses for the third time. "I was just as shocked as you."

"Well, it was sloppy. You should've been more explicit with your instructions."

"It's done... The question is what do we do next?"

"We see what Chinn Ho Lin has for us," Ward said. "No doubt Jefferson delivered something important. Otherwise we wouldn't be meeting today."

"I still don't like it. What if the Five find the Mongoose before we do?"

"Walter, we are two of the Big-Five. There's nothing to worry about, we just continue to take the lead as we have been. The other three will follow along."

Walter Kobayashi saw the wisdom in his old friend's tactics. The Big-Five families provided the perfect cover. The Mongoose had grievously harmed and relentlessly hounded the families for many years. It was perfectly natural that they would take action on their own. They had even notified the HPD of their investigation with the promise that if they found any evidence of the Mongoose's identity or whereabouts, they would promptly share it.

"It just makes me nervous to know that so many are looking for him," Kobayashi said, wiping his glasses again.

Jonathan Ward looked at his aging friend, Kobayashi. He had lost his bravado and confidence over the last few years. He wondered if perhaps he was getting older and more feeble himself. He couldn't let that happen, this was a dangerous game. Everything was riding on finding the Mongoose first. They needed to concentrate and act decisively.

"The HPD know nothing. They are waiting to hear from us. Jefferson apparently found some valuable information, but we've taken care of him," Ward said. "Once we get what we need from Lin, perhaps we should tie up that loose end as well."

"You're not serious, are you?"

"We have to do what's necessary to protect ourselves and our families."

Walter Kobayashi didn't respond immediately. He cleaned his glasses and sipped his hot tea carefully. Both men looked out the window at the beautifully rain drenched gardens.

"He knows too much already," Ward said forcefully.

Kobayashi nodded.

"What about Doctor Spencer and his PI friend, Costelilia?" Kobayashi asked. "We just can't kill everybody that's interested in the Mongoose."

"That vegetable and his PTSD buddy... They are clever, but we are more connected and have more resources. I have complete confidence in our efforts," Ward said. "We're motivated. We have a reason to find this weasel. They're just in it for the thrill and excitement of cracking a cold case."

"What if the Mongoose sold or destroyed the box? What if he opened it already and found the documents?"

"If the Mongoose found the documents already, I'm sure we would've been contacted by now. Blackmail is a convenient way to make millions," Ward said. "If the box was sold, we persuade him to retrieve it. If it was destroyed, that's even better."

"You seem to have an answer for everything," Kobayashi said.

"And you, my friend, have too many questions and worries."

Without further discussion, Kobayashi made a second call to the hit man.

Chapter 27

Chinn Ho Lin left the Pacific Club reluctantly. He was not a member, but he thoroughly enjoyed the atmosphere of the place and the excellent service. His application had been rejected several times. Apparently, his family was just not wealthy or well-known enough to merit membership. He imagined the deals and sales that he could make with access to the political and financial power brokers that frequented the club.

He jogged to his car in the parking lot. It was still raining and valet parking was for members only. The meeting had gone as well as expected. He had been nervous and in awe of the State's most powerful men, but he held his own and thought he had made a good impression.

It was his first time to meet all the Big-Five patriarchs at the same time. Milton Jiao, the current Chinese component of the group, he had met several times. They were partners in a few land deals and development projects. Their housing subdivision in Koolina was going very well. Jiao controlled the construction unions and had his hands in every major development project in the city. Walter Kobayashi had served at every level of government, and now ran the Democratic Party in Hawaii. They had met at political and war veterans' fundraisers. Kobayashi was his current contact with the Big-Five, and had arranged the meeting.

The other three, Jonathan Ward, Timothy Kahalalani and Richard Campbell, he had only seen at a distance or on television. Kahalalani was a large native Hawaiian, clearly uncomfortable given the surroundings. His family claimed to be ancestors of Kamehameha, giving the group some legitimacy with the Hawaiian people. Ward and Campbell were tall and slender, white-haired gentlemen who had inherited their wealth from huge family plantations established in the 19th century. They seemed to be the leaders of the group. All of the men were polite, but quick to get down to business.

"Welcome Chinn Ho, please sit down," Jiao said in Chinese. "Would you like some tea?"

"Yes, please."

"So, tell us what have you discovered about this pesky Mongoose?" Ward asked.

"The Mongoose is a woman, and we have her name."

"A woman?" Kobayashi asked. "Are you sure? The damage to our homes and offices doesn't seem like a woman." He nervously wiped his glasses in his lap, trying to conceal his sincere pleasure that his connection with Lin was paying off.

"It's definitely a woman. A local woman of Vietnamese-Hawaiian ancestry," Lin said.

"You said you have a name?" Ward asked.

"Mae-Linh Malia Nguyen Kawanakapili."

The five old men listened intently as he explained everything he knew about the woman—her father's death in the Bishop Towers construction accident, the fate of her brother and mother, her years of addiction, homelessness and crime, and her stint in prison."

"And where is she now?" Campbell asked.

"She was last seen on the Kawanakapili farm about twelve years ago."

"I asked where she is now," Campbell said, clearly irritated. In his experience, these meetings always went on too long, especially when the Asians he dealt with never gave straight answers.

"I'm sure if Mister Lin knew of her whereabouts, he would tell us," Jiao chimed in.

"She disappeared," Lin said. "But I'm sure that with the information we now have we can find her."

"Well, that's good news," Ward said.

Timothy Kahalalani remained silent. He seemed deep in thought.

"Timothy, do you have any questions for our friend?" Ward asked. Ward always tried to include the sweaty Hawaiian, if for no other reason than it was the politically correct thing to do.

"Well, yes, as a matter of fact I have a few. Where did this information come from? Is it reliable? How long do you think it will take to find this Mongoose? And, why was Michael Kalani Jefferson gunned down just outside your office immediately after his visit with you?"

The four patriarchs stopped sipping their beverages and gave each other knowing glances. Of the five, Kahalalani had the reputation for having the most scruples.

"Timothy, I can assure you Chinn Ho had nothing to do with that ghastly murder," Jiao said. "It was nothing more than a coincidence."

"A gang related murder I have been told," Kobayashi said.

"Yes, I had nothing to do with it. I was as shocked as everybody else. It's not every day someone gets shot down on our peaceful streets—after all we don't live in Chicago," Lin said.

"It seems to me that someone may be trying to protect the Mongoose," Kahalalani said, looking around the table.

Ward held up the envelope that Lin had given them. Silence blanketed the table.

"Enough of the cross-examination and needless defense," Ward said. "Chinn Ho has brought us more information than we've had in years. I suggest we take his word and act on his information as quickly as possible."

"Yes, good work Chinn Ho. Keep it up, we expect a report from you when you find her location," Kobayashi said.

"Thank you," Lin said. "I'll do my best."

"I'm sure you will," Ward said, dismissing the man.

Jiao had walked him out and slipped him a large fat envelope as they approached the front entrance.

"No worries, Chinn Ho that grumpy Hawaiian is always thinking there's some conspiracy going on. Keep up the good work, and call me the minute you find out anything new," Jiao said patting him on the back.

Chinn Ho felt the heavy envelope in the side pocket of his jacket. He loosened his tie and jumped into his silver Mercedes. He resisted the urge to count the money.

"Damn good day," he said to the rearview mirror, then thinking about the stalled construction at the Koolina subdivision—"If it would just stop raining."

He turned on to Queen Emma Street and headed towards Punchbowl. He made a full stop at School Street and prepared to turn left. A black SUV pulled up on his right. Chinn Ho, always a careful driver, looked left, and then looked right and left again before turning. Just before he put his foot back on the gas pedal, two hollow-point bullets passed through his brain shattering his skull and the drivers' side window. He was dead instantly. Blood began to pool on the leather headrest and flow down his back.

The driver of the SUV calmly got out of his car and walked around to the driver's side of the Mercedes. The heavy rain had no effect on him. He reached through the bloody, brain splattered broken glass of the side window, and put the car in park. He pulled the envelope from Lin's lifeless body and felt the weight of it. He snapped a picture with his iPhone and walked back to his SUV. He drove off into the Honolulu night. The downpour continued.

A damn good day, the hit man thought.

Chapter 28

The next morning, James began to analyze the crowd data again. To his frustration and relief, the rest of the previous day had been devoted to care giving chores—time on the toilet, a bath, changing the bed sheets, and a visit from the clinic nurse. He was frustrated not being able to continue the task-at-hand, but relieved that his mind had been taken off the bloodied corpse lying in the middle of the street.

He felt better. He was beginning to accept the consequences of his actions. The elimination of a notorious crime boss, vigilante justice, protecting a friend, they were all understandable motives, but when he saw Maggie's face in the crowd of onlookers, everything came into focus.

It was worth it.

If it had not been for the facial recognition software James would have never recognized her. Her disguise was convincing—she looked like any of the thousand nondescript blond haired, blue-eyed haole women living in the city. She looked a little older and rather plump, but after watching the video for a while, James definitely recognized the eyes and mannerisms of Maggie.

The software had brought up two possible matches— Mary Jay Higgins and Mae-Linh Malia Nguyen Kawanakapili. Within a few minutes, he had determined that Mary was an alias created by Maggie at least fifteen years ago. He immediately began an automated search to find out every piece of information in cyberspace regarding Mary Jay Higgins.

Did Maggie kill Jefferson?

James was thrilled and horrified at the same time to see the woman he had been searching for all of these years. His heart raced. The heart monitor alarm went off.

No, that's impossible. She is not a killer, but why was she there?

Lillian rushed into the room.

"Mister Spencer, are you okay? You must calm down."

"Thank you, I'm fine. Just got a little bit over excited."

Lillian shut off the alarms and gave him a pill to take the edge off.

James turned on the screen savers and closed his eyes. He let the OxyContin take over for a while. It felt good. He woke up an hour later to the sound of Lou's voice in the living room.

"You look ravishing my dear, younger every time I see you," Lou said.

"You just say that to make an old lady blush," Lillian laughed.

"Blush with desire!"

James smiled. He was used to this friendly banter between his best friend and Lillian. It was harmless fun and they had a genuine friendship. One of the things James enjoyed the most about Lou was his willingness to engage almost anyone in conversation. Lou had become more extroverted since the upgraded implants had calmed his PTSD. His sense of humor had heightened as well.

"How's the genius today?"

"He's doing pretty good, looking forward to seeing you."

"Well, you take the rest of the evening off. Go dancing or on a shopping spree," Lou said. "I'll take him outside for some fresh air."

"Okay Lou, I will be back around 8 PM. Is that okay?"

"Sure, have fun."

Lou came sauntering into the bedroom.

"What's shaking? Wake-up let's get out and visit the world."

"Hey Lou, good to see you. I'd like to get out for a while, but we should talk first."

"Fire away! You know anything about Chinn Ho Lin getting whacked last night?"

"Pretty weird, two professional hits in the same day," James said. "Do you think it's the same guy?"

"Probably so, my guess is Jefferson was killed after visiting Chinn Ho. Then he was cleaned up afterwards...Collateral damage."

"My thoughts exactly, it was Jefferson's men who ransacked my apartment, and I have some circumstantial evidence linking Jefferson to Lin."

"You said they were after anything you had on the Mongoose," Lou said. "Why?"

"Jefferson was working for Lin, and Lin was working for the Big-Five."

"You're kidding me... Those old families are involved in this."

Lou took his seat next to the bed.

"It makes sense. The families want the Mongoose stopped," James said. "She's been a nuisance for a long time."

"Then, who ordered the hits? It doesn't make sense that the Big-Five would take out their own operatives."

James remained silent for a few moments. He'd made the same conclusions and he was afraid to share the rest with his friend.

"Spit it out," Lou said. "You're hiding something from me."

"I think I might be responsible for the hits. I knew that Jefferson was getting close to learning the identity and possibly the location of Maggie. So, I arranged for a little bit of turmoil within his organization."

Lou leaned forward, "What exactly?"

"I manipulated some data so that it looked like Jefferson was embezzling from his own organization."

"Stealing from his bosses, that would get the biggest fish whacked," Lou said." Nice work."

"But, I didn't want to get anybody killed. I was just trying to distract them long enough so that we could find Maggie first."

"Mission accomplished," Lou said. "Don't give it another thought."

"That's easy for you to say, you're used to this kind of thing," James said, immediately regretting his comment.

"Yeah, you're right. I've done my fair share of killing, and when it's justified you just gotta learn to live with it."

Lou stood up and rubbed James' chest, a rare show of affection.

"Jimmy, you have saved thousands of lives. You didn't order the hits or pull the trigger."

James appreciated his friend's words and actions, but he knew it would take some time before he came to terms with his involvement.

"Let's go outside and enjoy the garden," Lou said. "You need some sunshine."

"I've got something else to show you," James said.

"You're full of surprises today!"

James switched his primary computer on and played the video for Lou.

"The crowd footage," Lou said. "Anything interesting?"

James stopped the video when it landed on Maggie. "Recognize this woman?"

164

"Looks a bit like a dancer at the club Roxy. Settin' up a date for me?"

"This is Mary Jay Higgins."

"Nice name, looks a little plump for me, but I'll give it a shot," Lou said laughing.

"Look closer, look at the eyes, mouth, chin... It's Maggie."

Lou remained uncharacteristically silent. He stared closely at the screen. James brought up the facial recognition data and showed James the two possible matches.

"Mary is Maggie's alias. She created Mary in 1995 or 1996 as far as I can tell."

"Holy shit."

James let the totality of their discovery sink in.

"Very clever girl," Lou said. "So, what next?"

"I'll track Maggie through her alias. I've already started gathering data on Ms. Higgins."

"And?"

"And you pay a visit to Chinn Ho Lin's office. We need to know how much he knew and how much has already been passed to the Big-Five."

Chapter 29

Maggie sat comfortably in the living room area of her lair, nestled safely in the center of the interconnecting munitions tunnels. The cool air of the cave was a pleasant respite from the oppressive heat outside. So far, it had been an eventful day—the hit on Jefferson in the afternoon and then the murder of Chin Ho Lin in the early evening just before the six o'clock news, occupied her thoughts. The connection between the men was not immediately apparent to her, but two murders in one day—that was unheard of in the peaceful city of Honolulu.

The cops will be working overtime...

She opened the hand written report from the canary she had at the Pacific Club. He was reliable and adept at listening carefully to Honolulu's elite, gathering interesting and useful information. With her eyes and ears throughout the city, Maggie always had her finger on the pulse of the islands. Today's report was particularly relevant. The canary had overheard a revealing conversation between Jonathan Ward and Walter Kobayashi, both members of the so-called Big-Five families.

She opened the report and squinted at the atrocious, but readable handwriting. The Mongoose demanded written reports delivered by couriers, just one of the many precautions she took to keep her cyber-footprint as small as possible. As soon as she got through the first couple of sentences, she realized that this was important information that would require decisive action.

Ward and Kobayashi were working rogue, outside the knowledge of the Big-Five. She already knew that the families were looking for her, but to know that these two powerful men had their own motivation to find and eliminate her was a revelation. Their operatives were most likely behind the murders of Jefferson and Lin. Maggie now understood that she was up against some very determined and dangerous adversaries. She was running out of time. *They will find me soon.*

The report told her that a family heirloom, a small jewelry chest, she had collected from the Kobayashi family estate over a year ago, had some sensitive documents hidden inside. The documents implicated several Ward and Kobayashi family members in a massive cover-up regarding the deadly Bishop Towers construction accident. The documents contained evidence of the negligence, the cover-up, and the bribes and blackmail that extended to the highest levels of government and the private sector.

Maggie gasped audibly when she read this news.

The bastards.

Her father had died in that accident and her family had been coerced into accepting a pittance of a compensation package—one that stipulated no further disclosures, investigation or lawsuits. Maggie remembered distinctly arguing with her mother and her uncles about the terms of the agreement, but they were the adults of the family and they were under pressure that she did not understand as a child. She believed, even then, that someone should be held responsible for her father's death. To know now there was a conspiracy, and that the Ward and Kobayashi families were behind it, made her heart race.

My father's death could have been prevented, she thought. *It should have never happened...*

Maggie thought about Luke's death as well. Another death that could have been prevented. Her anger welled up and fueled her resolve.

"I'll make them pay," she said to the walls of her cave.

Maggie understood she was a clear threat to these families. They were making every effort to find her and retrieve the documents before anyone else.

"I've got to find this jewelry box," she said heading towards the back of her living room.

Everything that she didn't sell or give away from her robberies was neatly stacked and organized in one of the adjoining tunnels. She grabbed a powerful flashlight and exited through a side door into the storage area. As she walked through the dark hallways of the caves, shining her light on shelves containing the booty of the past eighteen years, she tried to remember the jewelry box.

That was almost two years ago—an easy job, in and out within twenty-six minutes.

She could not remember the box at all.

That's good, it means that I didn't sell it, I would remember that. I probably just put it on a shelf and forgot about it.

A few minutes later, she found the shelf with the treasures from the Kobayashi mansion. The jewelry box was about the size of a large shoebox, made of rose wood and mahogany. It was intricately inlaid with pearl and ivory. The box was empty. She brought it back to her workstation off the living room and began to dismantle the cover, bottom and sides. She wielded her razor blade, hammer and screwdriver with her usual skill. The box, even though it was clearly a valuable Ward family heirloom from the early 19th century sugar plantation days, meant nothing to her.

Clever, she thought as she opened the false bottom that held the pages.

The box was beautifully made, and no doubt worth a nice sum. However, she proceeded to smash the box to bits—it was the only way to be certain she had gotten everything. It also seemed to be most appropriate and satisfying.

The documents she found were astounding. She found hand-written letters and memos to and from Kobayashi and Ward describing their thoughts and actions regarding the Bishop Towers construction accident. They were written in fountain pen ink on yellowing paper. The correspondence came from a time well before cell phones and e-mail.

She found a list of government officials and judges that had been bribed, along with a ledger indicating who was paid and the exact amounts. There were Xerox copies of letters indicating blackmail to a select few that had not accepted bribes, and copies of memos from attorneys and legal consultants marked confidential. There were even copies of building inspectors' reports with hand written notations in the margins indicating where changes should be made. The negligence leading up to the accident, as well as the cover-up was thoroughly documented.

Someone put this together to protect themselves, Maggie thought. *There is enough evidence here to place several people behind bars for many years.*

"Justice for my father's memory," she whispered, speaking directly to her ancestors.

Slowly, move carefully now.

She forced herself to breathe, to relax. She sat down in a large leather lounge chair and sipped the sweet iced tea she always kept close-by. She dimmed the lights in her cave.

Maggie realized that she needed to find out how close the Big-Five were to finding her. If they were too close, she may have to act quickly and disappear forever. If they were still clueless, it would give her more time to think things through and perhaps deliver a fatal blow.

Her first thought was to pay a visit to the Ward or Kobayashi offices and estates to find the information that Jefferson had passed on to them, but they were on high alert. Hitting them now would be nearly impossible.

Too risky, she thought.

She was unable to relax. She rose from the lounge chair, gathered up the documents and moved decisively to the very back of her lair.

Multiple copies with appropriate instructions need to go out. But, to who?

"Perhaps it's time to pay a visit to Chinn Ho Lin's office," she said as she put the documents into a worn leather satchel that had been hanging from a peg next to her office safe.

She knew the cops had already searched the Bishop Towers offices, but they would have been looking for clues to his murder, not information about the Mongoose. Surely, the Chinese realtor would have made some notes about his agreement with Ward and Kobayashi. That's where she might find her out how much the Big-Five knew, how close they were, and how much longer she had to continue operating.

By tomorrow evening, things would be back to normal. HPD would be on to something else.

I'll take a look then.

Chapter 30

It was a real treat for James to take a walk-ride in the garden and the neighborhood around the condominium. Lillian and Pablo sometimes took him out, but making the foray with Lou was always more enjoyable. They made a conscious effort to talk about things other than work. Every neighbor, jogger, dog owner, security guard, and maintenance worker greeted them. Lou joked that they were part of the neighborhood watch team. James smiled and made a few comments while Lou chatted with everyone.

James noted that Lou was in a particularly good mood today. Since the kidnapping and his recovery, Lou had switched his status with the Governor's security team to part-time. He was sleeping more and was less stressed. This change, along with the upgraded implants, had nearly eliminated all of his PTSD symptoms. He had reported to James that his thinking was clearer, and that he was having less anxiety and fewer recurring dreams. The second implant, the one that allowed them to stay connected, was also working very well.

When they got to their favorite spot, a comfortable couch at the far end of the condominium lobby with a lovely view of the pool, surrounding trees and garden, the two men suddenly grew quiet. They were thinking about Maggie.

"What are you doing?" James asked.

Lou was furiously typing on the tiny keyboard on his iPhone.

"Updating my contact list," Lou replied from the couch. "What is Buddy's master's name again?"

"You mean the Beagle mix?"

"Yeah."

Lou kept a list of nearly everyone he met on his phone. He understood the power of remembering people's names. Calling a person by their first name created an instant bridge of respect, putting people at ease. This was something he had learned as a leader of soldiers in the Marines—superiors were always "Sir", while subordinates were addressed by first name or a well-deserved nickname.

"Laura, her husband works in advertising," James answered.

Lou added pertinent information about each person, just little tidbits to jumpstart their next conversation.

A cool breeze blew through the lobby. The large trees around the pool and garden area threw shadows on the ground. The scent of tropical flowers wafted on the air. They both smelled a hint of Ginger coming from the flowers along the banks of Nuuanu Stream. The men stayed quiet, both lost in their own thoughts of Maggie.

Lou still had a nostalgic love for Maggie. She had been his first love, and perhaps his most powerful. He had never forgotten her. When he dreamed of embracing a woman, it was always Maggie. He had had other affairs and girlfriends, but the life of a Marine who constantly sought active deployments did little to promote long-term relationships or love. His PTSD didn't help either. Now, she had reentered his life—although, strangely and violently. He knew it was foolish to entertain thoughts of reuniting with her, but he couldn't help himself.

When Luke died, Maggie had fallen into an unresponsive and combative depression. Lou was unable to console her. Neither of them had been mature enough to understand the entire situation. Emotions, raw and uncontrolled, consumed their lives. Lou had never felt so confused. He wanted to hold her, to comfort her, but she pushed him away. After graduation from high school, joining the Marines and escaping the islands seemed to be his only way out.

Now, he felt some of those emotions coming back to him. Lou wanted to run away again, he sensed the danger, but he was still inexplicably drawn to her. These returning thoughts and feelings reminded him of when PTSD controlled his life. He looked at James in the wheelchair beside him and smiled, he was grateful for the implant he had given him. It allowed him to deal realistically with the complex reactions occurring in his head.

James returned his smile.

James also loved Maggie, but they had never been lovers. He'd been jealous of his bigger, athletic and more handsome best friend, but Maggie's capacity to share platonic love and her wonderful depth of feeling for life and nature had been more than enough to keep James happy. He felt special when he was alone with her, and fulfilled when he was with both of them. They understood each other completely. The three of them had shared a powerful bond that only teenagers wrapped in the emerging fantasy of lasting friendship and romantic love could fully experience. He wondered if that bond could be renewed.

James had fallen in love with a few other women. He'd married and divorced twice. His first marriage occurred while he was in residency and lasted less than two years. His second wife stayed with him much longer, but finally left him a couple of years before he was diagnosed with ALS. She had taken their son, which devastated him. She moved to Nevada to be close to her family. They had stayed in touch for the sake of the boy, but they had each moved on to pursue their own lives.

He understood why the women in his life abandoned him. He was driven by his work and the deep desire to save injured minds to the detriment of all else. He'd even rather repair other minds than his own. Sadly, this knowledge and pursuit, at times an obsession, was not applicable to repairing the ways of the heart. He wondered if Maggie would understand.

"Hey, why so quiet?" Lou asked.

"Just enjoying the fresh air," James said.

"You haven't said much about finding Maggie," Lou commented.

"Neither have you."

"What are we going to do?"

"I don't know."

When they arrived back at the penthouse, Lou made some pizza for dinner while James checked some messages on his laptop. Pizza was strictly forbidden by Lillian and his doctors, but Lou thought it was good to indulge with pizza and beer every so often. He made sure his friend took small bites and didn't choke. James loved the feeling of doing something forbidden—something normal, and the beer mixed well with his medications, creating a nice buzz.

"Well I'll be damned," James said.

"Interesting phrase coming from you, the beer must be kicking in."

"Oh yeah, but better yet, we just received another encrypted message from Maggie!"

"All right then, she must be thinking of us," Lou said.

It took a couple of minutes for James to decode the message. He read it several times and then gave the laptop to Lou.

The message was written in the reflection of the muddy waters of Jackass Ginger Falls.

Lou should be feeling better by now. Sorry, about the stupid cops— You'd think a dozen vases creating a perimeter would give some indication that perhaps the bomb squad should be called in. My previous advice still stands—back off and stand clear. M

"I believe she's serious."
"At least she has a sense of humor," Lou said.

Chapter 31

The Mongoose stayed in the shadows. The sheer concrete walls of downtown Honolulu swallowed up her slim figure. She slipped past the Bishop Towers security guard and began to scamper up the 46 flights of stairs to Chinn Ho Lin's office. It was dark in the stairwell. She turned on her Maglite, giving off just enough light to see a few feet in front of her. She was in excellent shape and expected to climb the 700+ steps in less than twenty minutes.

The darkness and the stairs reminded Maggie of one of the last weekend hikes she had taken with her father and brother—the two-hour march up the 3922 steps of *Haʻikū Ladder*[28] on the Windward side of the island.

They had climbed the ladder before, but her father wanted them to experience the sunrise over Kaneohe Bay. Both children had protested when their father woke them up several hours before dawn, but once they were on the road, the complaints stopped. Maggie and Luke knew that cooperation was worth the effort—their father's weekly excursions were always exciting and memorable, and if they were attentive, *Shave Ice*[29] from Hasagawa General Store would be their reward at the end of the day.

Luke bounded ahead as they climbed the sharp incline in the dark. He didn't go far, always stopping and waiting until they caught up. On a typical hike, her adventurous brother would roam far ahead, but the steep dangerous stairs and the cold wind kept him close. Maggie preferred to stay with her father. When he stopped to feel the air, she rested. When he touched a leaf or smelled a flower, she mimicked his actions. When he spoke, she listened.

---

[28] A.k.a. Stairway to Heaven
[29] Snow cone

"The clouds are moving over the mountains," he said as they stood at the first landing. "Come, the sunrise should be clear."

Moving steadily up the stairs of Bishop Towers, Maggie could still hear his words. She felt oxygen rich blood flowing through her muscles and vital organs. Like that day on the mountain, she felt alive. She had purpose.

I do this for you father, and for you too Luke.

The hard dry concrete steps of the dark stairwell disappeared behind her. She let her thoughts take her back to the moisture laden wooden stairs ascending the Koʻolau Mountains.

A little over two hours after they had started their hike, the small family made it to the top. Huddled together against the cool morning breeze, they watched the sky slowly brighten—gray, pink, red-orange, and then the sun was over the horizon. Like her father had promised, the clouds disappeared and the mountain mist evaporated. They had a clear view for miles in every direction. The cliffs and valleys below them grabbed at the light, reflecting a jungle filled with deep, rich, emerald green foliage.

The ocean in the distance also absorbed the sunshine.

Maggie remembered her father pointing to Kaneohe Bay and asking, "Do you see all of the colors in the Bay?"

Maggie was older and could recite his lessons well even then…"Aquamarine, turquoise, cobalt—"

"Sky blue, green—" Luke shouted, not wanting to be left out.

Maggie interrupted and quickly rattled off..." Sapphire, Navy blue, violet, lime green—"

Luke countered with, "light blue, brown..."

"Brown's not a color of the water, that's the reef," she had said.

Luke looked to his father for reassurance, "Dad, the reef is part of the sea too...it counts, doesn't it?"

Maggie understood the magic of the moment, so before her father could answer, she gave in to her little brother.

"You're right, Luke. The reef is part of the ocean, brown is a good color."

Maggie had been an understanding older sister. She loved her little brother. *I miss him still*, she thought as she took another flight of stairs.

"Dad, tell us the Hawaiian word for blue?" Luke had asked.

"Again? You don't remember..." Her father had said with his deep baritone voice.

"*Uli* is blue," Maggie said.

"Yes, and *uliuli* is the blue of the deep sea, but the Hawaiian people have many words for blue, just like in English."

The children moved closer. They paid attention to their father's lessons. English was their first language. It was the language their parents spoke with each other and the language they needed to master for school, but Hawaiian was spoken on the farm and at family gatherings. Hawaiian was special to them—it was their father's language.

"If the ocean is very dark, purple-blue, then we call it *pōpolohua*."

"pōpolohua..." Both children repeated.

"Then there is the saying, *Kai pōpolohua mea a Kāne,* which describes the ocean as the purplish-blue reddish-brown sea of *Kāne*.[30]"

"I like that the best," Luke said. "It puts them all together."

---

[30] Hawaiian religion has four main deities: Kāne, Kū, Lono and Kanaloa.

"Me too," Maggie had agreed.

Their father held them close, including his children in the special bond he felt with the land and the ocean.

"You see the Marine barracks in the distance," he said, pointing with his massive arms. "They are going to build a highway from there, through the valley just below us, under the mountain and over to the leeward side."

The children could see the Marine base at the far end of Kaneohe Bay, and Kailua town in the distance. The landscape before them was mostly green. The dominant features were the towering mountains and the expansive ocean surrounding the islands, but housing developments were slowly taking hold. Windward Mall, one of Luke's favorite places, was just below them. Traffic noise carried by the wind from Likelike highway reached their ears.

"Why? We got two highways through the mountains already?" Maggie had asked.

"There's no good reason," her father replied. "But Senator Inouye thinks it will be good for our island, good for the economy, good for the military and the people."

"Can they go through the mountain?" Luke asked.

"They say they can with great big machines and dynamite."

"*Pele*[31] will be angry," Maggie said.

Her father laughed and gave her an extra hug.

"Yes, you're right Malia, but I don't think even the great Pele can protect the *aina*[32] from this project. Your aunties and uncles are doing everything they can to stop it, but the government is too powerful. The road will come."

When Maggie reached the 46th floor, she stopped and rested for a minute. Her father had been right—the road did finally come. The concrete surrounding her smelled dank.

---

[31] The Hawaiian god of fire, the god of volcano
[32] The land

She felt entombed. The air was stale. In this dark tight space, the relentless pace of progress and development pressed in on her. The magic of the mountains was far away. Maggie remembered the mixture of reverence and sadness in her father's voice as he reminded them to rejoice in the nature around them and to respect the land. She felt his presence.

I will go for a hike in the mountains soon.

She took off her backpack and prepared the necessary equipment to disable the motion detectors and video monitors in the hallway just beyond the stairwell door. She was ready. She was hopeful that she would find what she needed in Lin's office.

Yes, father, I do this for you.

Chapter 32

Lou didn't particularly like breaking and entering, but with the assistance from the voice in his head, it was relatively easy.

"This first door leads to the stairwell," James said. "Use the three-gauge pick."

"Roger."

"There are no alarms until you get to the inner hallways."

James immersed himself in the visual, auditory, and kinetic information transmitted to his control room as Lou made his way up to the 46th floor. The holographic and three-dimensional aspects of his system were sharper and more detailed with the upgraded implants. James believed he could feel the hardness of the concrete steps and the cool moisture condensing on the cement walls. Enhanced night vision made everything crystal-clear and the upgraded surround-sound listening capacity allowed him to hear every step and breath that Lou made.

"Eighteen floors to go," James said.

"Easy for you to say," Lou responded, clearly fighting for breath.

"I think I'll get you a Stairmaster for Christmas."

"And, I'll buy you a new pair of legs."

James stayed quiet after that and directed his nervous energy to checking all of the recording and experiential systems, and testing their enhancements. The newly installed microwave transmitter in Lou's shoulder was sending out strong GPS data. Everything seemed to be working perfectly.

He switched to the infrared spectrum. Detection of thermal signatures was working well, although there was little to look at in the stairwell. The olfactory sensors picked up the odor of Lou's sweat, which was dominant, but James also detected the smell of steel, concrete, discarded food, and the hint of some kind of flowery perfume. It may have been Ginger or Jasmine. He guessed that whoever had passed by earlier, perhaps a female security guard, had been wearing the fragrance. James detected a metallic taste in Lou's saliva. He checked Lou's body temperature and blood pressure. His friend was on the verge of over exhaustion.

"Okay, now what," Lou asked standing in front of the 46th floor stairwell door.

"Take a break," James said. "Did you bring some Gatorade or something?"

"No, why?"

"You're heart rate is up. I can taste iron, you're sweating...you need to drink—"

"You know too damn much," Lou said. "Just turn off the fuckin receptors if I'm bothering you."

"Okay, okay..."

James let Lou catch his breath, "When you're ready use the security scan card I gave you," James began again. "It should open the door and not set off any alarms, but once you're inside hug the left wall. Remember there is a motion sensor top-right that we need to disable before you proceed."

"10-4..."

Lou steadied himself. He consciously took deep cleansing breaths as his *Sin Moo Hapkido* Master had taught him. He focused on the meridians throughout his body, especially his tired legs. Once he felt his *Ki* restored, he slipped into the hallway and slid along the wall until he was underneath the motion sensor. He shined his pen light at the small plastic box. To his surprise, it was already covered by a piece of black cloth.

"Jimmy Boy, do you see what I see?"

"Yes, very strange. It seems that someone was here before you and did not clean-up after themselves."

"Or, that someone is still here."

"I'm not detecting anything," James replied.

Lou proceeded towards Chinn Ho's office. He stopped and checked the motion sensors and closed-circuit video cameras on his way down the long hallway. Each one had been neatly covered with small strips of adhesive black cloth.

"Black velvet, how luxurious," Lou said.

"And convenient...be careful."

For a minute, Lou wasn't sure if the last words he had heard were from his own voice, or the voice in his head. He stood in front of the Chinn Ho Lin's office door and took note of his adrenaline level, blood pressure and racing heart. The door was large and wooden. It reminded him of something—something unpleasant.

He suddenly flashed back to the night in Afghanistan at Camp Eggers about a week before he was discharged. He had found himself outside of the compound, fully geared up and ready for a firefight. With his night-vision goggles, he scanned the surrounding area. His M-16 was loaded—the safety was off. Four hand-grenades were clipped to his vest. He was jacked-up.

He was standing in front of an Afghan house. His consciousness was overwhelmed by a fog created by the contraband alcohol he had consumed earlier in the evening while attempting to drown the memories of his recent TBI. He had no idea how he got there, or why, but he had an uncontrollable urge to break down the door and kill everyone inside.

Why?

He stood in front of the doors in the Bishop Towers office building and tried to remember why, even though it was long ago. Why he'd had the urge to kill, to hurt, to extract some revenge... Why he still had those same urges?

Sure, the Taliban had emerged from walled houses with large wooden doors just like the one he was standing in front of...but, that was after the IEDs had stopped his unit. That was in the heat of battle, in Arghandab Valley—not the streets of Kabul, not Honolulu.

"Lou, are you still with me?"

"Yep, yeah Jimmy... I'm still here," Lou answered.

"The scan card should work for this office as well," James said. "Ready when you are."

James' voice was reassuring. It had a calming effect. Lou didn't answer right away. Instead, he cleared his thoughts and remembered.

He remembered that a voice, not James', had stopped him that night from breaking down the door and murdering a house full of innocent Afghans. It was the voice of his most trusted Sergeant. The Sergeant had followed his senior officer out of the compound out of curiosity, as well as out of a sense of duty to protect his drunken brother from harm. The Sergeant recognized what was about to happen, talked him down, and brought him safely back to the base. It was then that Lou realized that he'd had enough—it was time to seek an honorable discharge. His life as a Marine was over.

"Going in," Lou said.

"Gotcha covered."

The office was pitch-black. According to James' research and surveillance, there were no alarms or cameras to worry about—the cameras inside the office were turned-on manually and during the day only. Using only his penlight, Lou made his way to Chinn Ho's office.

"Lou, someone's in the office...," James said.

Lou froze and reached for his Glock.

"Infrared reading indicates a person at your three o'clock."

Lou knelt to the floor and aimed his gun and his flashlight in the direction James had indicated.

"Better show yourself you bastard, hands up away from your body or I'll empty my clip," Lou said.

A wooden chair smashed across Lou's back. His flashlight and Glock went sprawling across the floor. The wind was knocked out of him, but he managed to roll over. With a sweeping motion, he took the legs out from under the assailant. He heard a groan as the person's head slammed against the coffee table. Lou took his moment of advantage and pounced on top of the attacker's torso, flipping him over and quickly tying his hands behind his back.

"Lou, are you all right?"

"Busy right now, but everything is okay. I got this dude under control," he said keeping his weight on.

"It's not a dude," James said.

Lou held the person down while he grabbed a glow stick from his vest pocket. He snapped it and the room was quickly awash with a dim greenish light.

"Well I'll be damned," Lou said. "He didn't feel quite right, a little too soft and small to be a man."

Lou found his penlight and holstered his Glock. He flipped the woman over and shined his flashlight in her face. She had a nasty gash on the side of her head, but her eyes were wide open.

"Maggie?" James and Lou said at the same time.

She didn't answer at first, but blinked as if clearing her head.

"It is you," Lou said.

"Yes, it's me you big hulk. You've gained weight...you're fat, get off me. I can barely breathe," she said.

He thought about it for a moment.

"No yelling, fighting, or biting... Okay?" Lou asked, before he moved.

189

"Be careful, don't trust her. She's already caused us enough trouble," James said.

"I'll be careful," Lou replied, as he lifted his weight off her.

"Don't do it!" James shouted.

"Don't shout."

Maggie gave Lou a perplexed look, "Who are you talking to?"

"What?" Lou said, straddling the woman's body. He was still trying to comprehend the situation—not knowing which voice to answer.

"Okay, perhaps it is time for us to talk," she said pushing him aside.

Lou grunted his agreement and then helped her off the floor.

They sat on the leather couch—one on each end.

"I don't like it, but where do we start?" James asked inside Lou's head.

"Good question," Lou answered.

"Why are you talking to yourself? Are you wired or something?" Maggie asked. "Is it true that you have some kind of mind control connection with Spencer?" She looked at him with a mixture of surprise and relief. Blood trickled from her forehead down her cheek.

"I guess I'll start first," Lou said, grinning, thinking that it was still the same "in-charge" Maggie after all of these years.

"I have an implant in the back of my head, well actually two implants. One controls my PTSD symptoms, and the other allows me to connect remotely with James. He can see, smell and hear everything I can. Probably more than that, but I'd rather not know all of his capabilities."

"So it is true... I'm not sure what to think. It sounds horrifying, like something out of a Star Trek episode."

"It is true, and yes, parts of it are a little weird, but it works," Lou said. "And, the implants have helped me a lot."

"So, he can hear me?"

"Yep, he can see you too..."

"Hello Jimmy!" Maggie said.

"I can't believe it's you," James replied.

"He says hello back," Lou said. "Your turn to give us something, like... What are you doing here?"

"Untie me?"

"No," James said.

Lou ignored him, reached behind her back and removed the plastic ties holding her wrists together. The soft scent of her hair and the heat coming from her body was intoxicating. He smelled Ginger. After thirty years, she still held that power over him.

"I'm here, trying to find out how much Chinn Ho Lin gave to the Big-Five. Of course you know that they are after me," she said.

"Did you kill Hammerhead Jefferson and Chinn Ho?" Lou asked.

"No, I don't kill, but I'm not sorry to see them gone."

"Ask her why the hell she kidnapped you and set off the IEDs," James said.

Before Lou could relay James' question, Maggie continued. "I'm sorry I had you picked up and beaten. I hope my guys didn't hurt you too badly. I had to send a message you would not ignore—James was getting too close to finding me."

"Tell her she did a good job," James said." And next time use a telephone."

Lou laughed.

"Why are you laughing?" Maggie asked.

"Well, it's strange. You just answered the question the voice in my head wanted me to ask you," Lou said.

"The voice in your head?"

"That'll be James, most of the time anyway."

Lou wasn't sure he liked carrying on a three-way conversation—with one person absent from the room.

"Tell James I'm sorry."

"Tell him yourself, he can hear you quite clearly," Lou said.

Maggie hesitated for a moment. It was bizarre enough talking to Lou, one of her best friends from high school in an office that she had just broken into, let alone talking to a virtual Jimmy through his head. She didn't know if she should run, or continue the conversation.

"I'm sorry Jimmy. I'm sorry I hurt you and Lou. I'm not the same person I was before. I don't expect you to understand or to forgive me."

"If Maggie didn't take out Jefferson and Lin, it means someone else is involved. Ask her about that?" James said.

"James wants to know who else could have set up the hits. He thinks someone else is involved. Tell us what you know," Lou said.

"It's way deeper than you can imagine... You two should walk away and not be involved. Just let me go, I'll take care of it myself," Maggie said.

"I think I can speak for both of us when I tell you that we've been looking for you as friends. We'd like to help you. We never intended to turn you over to the authorities or anyone else," Lou said.

"Do you agree, James?"

"Yes. Maggie has nothing to worry about, so long as she stops threatening us. I want to help her," James said.

Lou relayed James' words.

"Thank you," Maggie said.

"Signing off," Lou said.

"No Lou!" James yelled. "You can't be serious!"

The feed from Lou went black.

Chapter 33

James was furious. He tried to thrash violently in his bed, but managed nothing more than to swing his head back and forth. He wanted desperately to hit something or to throw an object at the wall. The alarms on his ventilator and heart monitor began to scream. Lillian came running into the room.

"Mister Spencer, what's wrong?"

James didn't answer. He just shook his head back and forth.

Lillian checked all of his ventilator hoses and connections—everything was working properly. She held his head still and tried to talk to James again.

He refused or could not respond, so she darted to the corner of the room and grabbed a syringe and a mild sedative from a small refrigerator. She quickly administered the medication.

"Mister Spencer, calm down... everything is okay," she said softly.

A few minutes later, he stopped thrashing and his heart rate and breathing returned to normal. He closed his eyes.

He fell into a deep dream.

He was walking in the sand at Waimanalo Beach—*yes, walking*. The crystal-clear water flowed over his ankles and bare feet, washing away the footprints he'd left behind. He looked further down the sugar white sand beach and saw the green gray-black cliffs of Makapuu in the distance. The sky was a perfect baby blue. The Tradewinds forced tiny cotton balls of clouds against the mountains. He followed a large white Swift with his eyes as the bird banked off the cliffs and turned towards Rabbit Island. He looked over the water towards Molokai sitting on the horizon.

He was mesmerized by the numerous shades of green and blue the reflected sunlight light created on the water. He spotted a sea turtle poking its head above the surface for a moment, and then it disappeared. He heard voices calling his name.

He turned and looked towards the wind-bent Ironwood Pines behind him. Lou, Maggie, Johnny, Shingo, Luke, and a few other friends were waving to him, telling him that the barbecue was ready. He started to jog towards the picnic table when suddenly the sand opened up and he fell through the Earth into the galaxy and universe beyond. He knew instantly that he would never return.

He was sad to have to say goodbye to his friends, but he was thrilled at the eternal majesty that now surrounded him.

Lillian stayed by his side while he slept.

Chapter 34

The professional hit man was also an excellent private investigator. His services were valued because he was equally adept at finding people, as well as eliminating them. He suspected that the Mongoose would show up at Chinn Ho Lin's office hoping to determine how much was known about her identity and whereabouts. He also astutely deduced that the Mongoose would appear sometime in the darkest few hours just before dawn—after zero dark thirty.

Spending a few nights waiting for his prey was no problem. Unlike many PI's and professional hit men, he didn't mind a stakeout. It wasn't boring for him to sit quietly for hours. He rather enjoyed the silence, especially since his patience usually paid off very well.

Tonight was no exception.

Just before 4:30 AM, the Mongoose emerged from the shadows and entered the Bishop Towers complex. He could have easily killed her then, but that would have only earned him 60% of his possible commission. He needed the documents and the kill to make the full 100% of what he had requested. Sixty percent of a quarter million dollars was a lot, but he was sure that with a little patience, he would succeed with both—the full $250,000 would be much more satisfying. He decided to follow the Mongoose, discover her secrets and then make his move.

To his surprise, however, seventeen minutes later, a large man also entered the Towers. The man was the same size and build as James Spencer's man, Lou Costelilia, but he could not be sure it was him—the dark shadows concealed his face. Chinn Ho no doubt had many enemies and even more secrets. There were probably at least a dozen powerbrokers willing to pay a burglar to search the realtor's office. It could be just about anyone.

His first inclination was to follow the man and stop him. He didn't need anyone interfering with the Mongoose's routine and current mission. He needed her to feel comfortable in her chosen environment. However, the chances of eliminating the man without creating some disturbance that would alert her to his presence, was slim. He reprimanded himself for not stopping the man before he entered the building. After a quick review of all of his options, he decided to lay low and let events play-out.

He sipped his coffee and waited.

At exactly 5:32 AM, the Mongoose and the man exited the building, together. In the grayish light of the earliest hours of the morning, he definitively identified the man as Lou Costelilia. He stored that information in case it was relevant later and didn't give him a second thought. Now, his goal was to follow the Mongoose without being discovered. He needed to focus all of his energy and considerable expertise on this task.

They said something to each other, embraced and then went their separate ways.

A driver was waiting for her in a back alley near South King Street. He followed the black SUV through the streets of Honolulu, Chinatown, Kalihi, and then finally on to the main highway heading west. He stayed well back, being sure not to raise any suspicion. Forty minutes later, he pulled off the potholed gravel road running through the Waikele Gulch and watched the car enter the front yard of a fenced in underground storage area.

The sun was high enough to shed some morning shadow onto the red earth walls of the narrow canyon. He left his car, climbed through the underbrush and up the sidewall of the gulch. From a hidden vantage point, he watched the Mongoose and her man as they parked the car in a cave-garage. They secured the perimeter of the storage area and then went into one of the tunnels.

He'd done enough for one morning. He would come back later and complete his surveillance before finishing the job.

He had found the Mongoose's lair.

Chapter 35

Campbell and Kobayashi sat quietly on a bench in the back garden of the Pacific Club. Their jackets and ties lay neatly on the wicker rocking chair in front of them. Both men were sweating and had opened their shirt collars to capture what little breeze there was. The air was heavily scented with a sticky sweet mixture of humidity, tropical flowers, and the odor of garlic shrimp coming from the nearby kitchen.

Kobayashi nervously wiped his wire-rimmed glasses over and over, trying to get the lenses clean—never successful. Campbell swatted at the numerous mosquitoes biting his sunburned arms, neck and exposed ankles.

"So your man has located the Mongoose," Campbell said. "Good."

"Yes, apparently she has some kind of den at the underground storage facility in Waikele," Kobayashi said.

"Seems fitting...when will he finish the job?"

"In the next day or two."

"Be sure to make your instructions clear. We don't need another messy job like Jefferson. We need it to be quiet and clean, no collateral damage," Campbell said squashing a blood-filled mosquito on his left arm. He left it there, as if making a point.

The blood made Kobayashi queasy. The iPhone image of Chinn Ho's shattered head and bloodied body came back to him.

"Yes, yes, I understand."

"We also want the documents. Then this whole debacle can be behind us," Campbell said.

"Just to be clear, the elimination is the priority, the documents are secondary. Do we agree?" Kobayashi asked.

"We need the documents. Before she is killed, your man should make every effort to find them. Is that clear enough?"

Kobayashi took off his constantly fogging glasses and wiped them again. He looked at his longtime friend.

"We're both getting old, Jonathan."

"Let's hope this is the last time we have to talk about this," Campbell replied. "For the sake of our grandchildren..."

Kobayashi nodded.

Chapter 36

Maggie knew what was up when her senior man called her to the garage. Calvin Kalaheo had been with her from the beginning when she had left the Kawanakapili farm. She called him Uncle Calvin even though they were not actually related.

He was the only native Hawaiian on her crew. He had known her father and mother. Calvin and her father had been best friends. They had struggled together to raise families and balance the traditional Hawaiian way of life with the modern reality of jobs, paychecks and bills.

Calvin understood Maggie's history. He was at the Bishop Towers construction site the day her father died, and he had watched over her ever since. He tried hard to keep some of the old traditions alive, make new ones, and give the group a sense of family. Maggie picked all of her men carefully. She trusted them explicitly, paid them well and welcomed them as part of the family, but Uncle Calvin was 'ohana.

"Okay, uncle, I'll be right there," she said into the intercom as she slid off the treadmill.

Maggie knew that Uncle Calvin had probably gathered together most of the guys to celebrate her birthday. He was an independent and competent mechanic. He rarely called her for any type of garage related consultation. The shop and all of the mechanical systems throughout the compound were his responsibility. Only the IT and surveillance systems were relegated to other, younger men.

Forty-seven, damn... Another year older, she thought.

Seeing Lou had also made her feel her age. While she dried off and changed clothes, she thought about their encounter the night before.

When Maggie had heard the large wooden door of the realtor's office open she immediately took cover in the darkest corner of the room. She watched the large man as he moved carefully through the reception area and came into Chinn Ho Lin's private office. It was the last thing that she had expected. She had never been interrupted on a job before. *Who is this idiot?* She had wondered.

The man was big and walked clumsily, bumping into furniture. He wasn't able to follow his own penlight. His eyes went in one direction, while his body moved in another. He was no professional burglar. He seemed to be distracted—he was whispering to himself.

She remembered watching, weighing her options. She could have sliced his throat with her razor blade before he even realized she was there, but that would have left a mess and she preferred not to kill an innocent person.

She decided to flee at the appropriate moment. There was nothing left for her to do in the office anyway. She had already found what she was looking for—the Big-Five were aware of her identity. Hammerhead Jefferson had gained valuable information from Spencer's apartment. They were getting closer.

What was this guy after? She had wondered.

The man had suddenly shined his flashlight in her direction, pulled his handgun and ordered her to stand still, but she was too quick. She had anticipated him, changed position, and came up behind him with an antique Koa wood chair—that she promptly smashed into his exposed back. The gun and the flashlight had gone flying.

She bolted for the door, but somehow the man was able to swipe her legs out from under her. She fell and smashed her head on a table. He pulled her towards him. To her surprise, he had quickly gained the advantage.

"Maggie, where are you?" Calvin said over the intercom.

"I'm on my way..." She looked in the mirror one last time and made sure she looked presentable. It was her birthday party after all. The gash on her forehead was healing. The bruises she had sustained were minor. The fact that she had been captured, even if it was Lou, bothered her immensely. She replayed each detail of the struggle.

She remembered fighting desperately. She had been furious at the man, and angrier with herself. He was at least a hundred pounds heavier and much stronger. He was not a burglar, nor a cop, but he knew how to fight. She was soon subdued and flipped on to her stomach with her hands tied behind her back. She was powerless. She hadn't felt so awkwardly helpless since she found herself being raped along the Ala Wai Canal. Her mind raced, trying to determine if there was a way out.

When he had finally turned her over, she greeted him with eyes wide open.

She had recognized him immediately in the greenish shine of the glow stick he had deployed. When he directed his penlight in her face and said her name, she couldn't speak. The blow to her head, and the humiliation of being tackled and held down, had disrupted the connections between her thoughts and her vocal cords.

She was not sure how to respond. Adrenaline still coursed through her veins. She forced herself to breathe underneath his heavy weight. She still wanted to flee, but the need to fight subsided. She calmed herself and looked in the eyes of the man holding her down.

It was Louis, Lou... He was much older and quite a bit heavier than she remembered, but his face still had the same humor and compassion. She remembered how much he was in love with her, and how she embraced his feelings while keeping a more mature perspective on their relationship. They had just been high school kids after all.

He lifted her onto the couch. He untied her. She relaxed and began to talk with him, and James—even though he wasn't really there. The words began to flow as if they had never skipped a beat—their friendship and special bond was still there after all of these years.

After a few minutes, Lou had made a passing gesture over the back of his head and said a few seemingly unrelated words.

"What was that?" She asked.

"What was what?" He replied.

"That thing you just did..."

"Oh, the *'signoff'* thing," Lou said. "I just disconnected with James. He'll be pissed off, but I thought it would be better if we continued our conversation in private."

Maggie had given him a perplexed look.

"James can no longer see or hear what I am experiencing. I no longer hear a voice in my head, well at least not Jimmy's voice."

"So it really works?"

"Quite miraculously actually, just a couple of tiny implants in the back of my head," Lou said turning around nonchalantly and bowing before her, pointing to the Kevlar patch covering the mechanisms.

Maggie had touched the back of his head, tentatively at first. Then, as the revulsion towards the invasive technology, the unnaturalness of it subsided, she stroked his head. She marveled at the thought that a mere five minutes ago, they were ready to kill each other, and now they were sitting comfortably on a couch chatting like two school chums. His gesture, the exposure of the back of his head and neck, suggested a complete trust—a sort of submission that a stallion might make to his mare. She was not aware how much she craved that feeling of trust.

"I'm not the Terminator or anything weird like that," Lou said.

Maggie laughed. She could see that the sound of her laughter brought a smile to Lou's face.

"Still it must be a little bit strange," she said.

"I've gotten used to it. And thanks to your henchmen and the beating they gave me, I now have upgraded implants and greater control over the connection with Jimmy."

"Again, I am sorry about that. There was really no other way. James was getting too close and the warnings and messages I had sent earlier seem to do no good. I knew that I could get to him through you."

"You sent warnings and messages previously?"

"Several over the last couple of years, but he kept digging."

Lou got up off the couch and brought a wet towel from the mini-bar. He wiped the gash on her forehead.

"Maggie, what happened to you?"

She remembered thinking at that moment how strange the sensation felt to want to tell him everything. A feeling of trust and closeness to another human being was present that she believed had escaped her forever.

She had told him her story.

"Long-story-short, after you left for the Marines I fell into the darkness of addiction, crime and prostitution. I never went back to school. Chinatown alleyways became my home—burglary and theft my way of life. That lasted several years until I wound up in the women's correctional center. Four years later, I came out drug free, but still lost. I readjusted to society while living with my relatives on Kawanakapili Farm. This lasted for a while, but then in the early 1990s, I became the so-called Mongoose."

207

"I never knew. James kept what he knew about you to himself. He never told me that he was looking for you. I thought you were lost, moved far away, or dead."

"What happened to you?" Maggie had asked.

"The Marines," Lou said. "Soldiering, deployment, and weekend passes became my life. I never married."

"I'm sorry."

"No need to be, I turned out okay. Several years ago, I was discharged with PTSD and James was able to help me out. Been hanging here ever since."

Maggie looked at her watch, the vibrating silent alarm had gone off a second time.

"It's getting late. We have to clean up and get out of here before the early commuters start to arrive."

"You're right," Lou said. "But Maggie, I want you to understand that I will help you do whatever it is that you need. I'm sure James feels the same way."

She looked at the sincere expression on his face, and then deep into his eyes.

"Thanks, I'll remember that."

They cleaned up the office, making sure there were no traces of blood, or their struggle, except for the broken chair. When they had finished, Maggie told Lou what she had found in the office files about Jefferson, Lin, and the Big-Five families. It was clear to both of them that the information was now probably in the hands of the Big-Five—they knew who she was. Lou had listened carefully, understanding the danger that she was facing.

Outside of the office, Maggie had sent Lou to the end of the hallway. Staying in the shadows, she quickly removed the strips of black cloth from each of the motion sensors. She deftly slipped under the sensors' range until she joined him at the stairway.

A few minutes later, they were outside of the building. Quite spontaneously, Maggie had given Lou a tight embrace. He had fumbled to return the gesture, but before he could get his arms around her, she was gone.

She remembered the embrace.

It had felt right.

The embraces that Uncle Calvin and her men gave for her birthday—also seemed to be right. The men towered over her. Their hugs smothered her. They were a mixed group of men, Hawaiians, Samoans, Micronesians—all local. All of them united under the leadership of this tiny slender woman on a mission. It was a mission that they didn't quite understand, but they accepted because of her fairness and skillful leadership.

The jokes were off-color, but respectful. The *haupia*[33] pudding, her favorite from Liliha Bakery, was sweet and cool. The sweet tea the men served was just right. The Ginger lei Uncle Calvin placed around her neck felt heavy and moist with aloha. The pungent aroma soon overpowered the smell of grease, oil and gasoline in their garage.

She felt safe. She knew that the men in her life were there to help her.

---

[33] Coconut pudding

Chapter 37

Later that evening, James finally answered one of Lou's calls. James had calmed down and Lou promised to come over so they could talk.

He burst into the apartment his usual cheerful self. Flirted harmlessly with Lillian for a few minutes and then made his way to the back bedroom where James was working.

"What you got going?" Lou asked, as if nothing had happened.

"Not much, just trying to identify the hit man who took out Jefferson, and probably Chinn Ho Lin."

"You think they're related?"

"Yep," James replied.

Lou could tell he was still angry. Not ready to talk.

"Can I help?"

"Sure, I got tons of video to sift through. You can look through the stuff Morimoto sent over—mostly traffic cams."

Lou turned on a secondary computer across the room and started up the video analysis program.

"We're looking for a clear shot of the face or the car," James said.

"Approximate time about 15:20, if I remember correctly," Lou said making himself comfortable in front of the computer monitor.

"Scan from about thirty minutes prior to thirty minutes after. He may have been following Jefferson or stayed around to watch afterwards."

"Morimoto and his guys didn't find anything?" Lou asked.

"Nothing definitive—just some blurry images of a large Caucasian man firing an automatic rifle from a black SUV."

The room grew quiet as both men concentrated on the task before them. They were both relieved to have something to do.

"So, are you going to ask me about Maggie?" Lou finally said.

"I thought you would tell me when you were good and ready."

"There's nothing to tell really."

"Come on Lou, then why the disconnection?"

Lou got up from his computer and came over to James' bedside.

"Sometimes I just need a little privacy. You know that Maggie and I had a special bond, and it was the first time I'd seen her in almost thirty years. What did you expect?"

"I expected you to not disconnect me. You were on the job, it wasn't like you two met for a date in a coffee shop or something," James said.

James turned off his monitor with a quick verbal command and looked at Lou.

"Chances of finding something useful in the video footage is pretty slim anyway, we are dealing with a professional," he said.

"Jimmy, look, nothing happened. We talked about old times and she told me a little bit about the last thirty years. I showed her my implants and told her about my time in the Marines."

"Showed her your implants, huh? Sounds pretty intimate."

"You're just jealous," Lou said.

"Maybe I am. She was my friend too."

"Okay, I can understand that, but I'm not going to apologize for disconnecting. That's my option now. We already had that discussion."

"Okay, okay, so did you learn anything new?"

"It seems like Jefferson and Chinn Ho figured out Maggie's true identity, but they know nothing about her alias, Mary Jay Higgins, or her location. We can assume the information has been passed on to the Big-Five."

"What does Maggie know?" James asked.

"She knows that they got the information about her identity from your apartment. She doesn't know that you know about Mary Jay Higgins."

"Does she need our help?"

"Yes she does, but she will not ask for it. She still wants us to back off the Mongoose's trail."

"Okay then, we'll back off the Mongoose, but we can still look for the hit man and investigate the Big-Five connection."

"Yeah," Lou said. "Perhaps we can stop them before they find Maggie."

"I hope so."

Chapter 38

The Hertz rental car, a red Toyota Corolla, was extremely uncomfortable. It drove like a Go-Kart and the air conditioning blew warm air. The hit man's gaudy Hawaiian shirt was moist with sweat. His khaki shorts were too tight. He squirmed in the small seat. He took another huge gulp of bottled water and cursed the traffic. It was midday and there were still cars bottlenecked at the H1 – H2 interchange.

"Probably an accident," he growled.

He took his ire off the traffic by reviewing the layout of the Mongoose's hideout in his mind. He had spent a large part of the previous day surveying the area and the movements of the Mongoose and her pups. It seems she rests during the heat of the day—she was most active in the early morning hours and the evening.

She had several men working for her in shifts of three—two on guard duty and one stayed close to the garage. The guards were Polynesian, ex-military. They provided security and patrolled the perimeter. They were well armed and careful. The other man was older and acted more like a handy man. He lived on the premises. He seemed harmless enough.

The Mongoose stayed inside her cave most of the time. Large steel doors kept the cool, dry air inside the tunnels from escaping, and the outside tropical heat at bay. The doors were his primary concern. Taking out the two security men would be no problem. Then he would force the handy man to open the doors, if not, he could always blow them. Once inside, he would play a game with the Mongoose that he was very good at—hide and seek, and then kill.

From the diagrams he had been able to find, he thought the layout of the tunnel system was fairly straightforward. They were originally storage bunkers for ammunition, but had been converted to commercial storage space in the 1980s. What modifications the Mongoose had made over the last twenty years were of little consequence. Once he was inside, there was no way that she could escape. He was confident—hot and uncomfortable, but confident.

"I think I'll take a trip to Iceland after this," he said to the noisy AC, fiddling with the dials.

About an hour later, he pulled up to the front gate of the storage facility. One of the security men stepped out of the shadows of a large tree and approached the Toyota. The cloud of red dust that had been following the small car overtook them, temporarily blocking out the blazing sun. The guard waved the dust away from his face and approached the car.

He rolled down his window and poked his puffy white face towards the security guard, his disguise as a lost tourist in play.

"Hey good buddy, I'm lost big time. Supposed to be at the 'why-key-lay' golf course thirty minutes ago," he said with an exaggerated Texan accent.

He kept his eyes on the approaching man, but searched peripherally for the other guard. He wanted to take them both out at the same time.

"You are definitely off track," the man said cheerfully. "We get lots of people down here that have taken a wrong turn."

"Damn, I knew I should've turned left back there," the hit man said.

"Yep, go back down the way you came. When you come to the stop sign turn right, go about three miles and then you'll see the sign for the *Wai-ke-le* golf course." The guard carefully pronounced the name of the golf course, hoping the tourist wouldn't continue to destroy it.

"Much obliged," he said. "You wouldn't have some cold water to spare, would you? I'm plum out and awfully parched."

He raised his empty water bottle out of the window.

The guard took a quick walk around the car. When he was satisfied that there was nothing suspicious about the car and the sweaty Caucasian, he opened the gate.

This was Hawaii after all, the land of aloha—got to keep the tourists happy.

"Park by that tree, I'll get you some water."

"Damn nice of you!"

He got out of the car and waited under the shade of the tree. He took a couple of pictures with the oversized camera around his neck and swatted at the flies buzzing around his lily-white legs. He wiped his face and arms with a cheap beach towel. He fiddled with the large fanny pack around his belly. He seemed completely out of his element.

The guards watched him from the garage and laughed. They had seen lots of crazy tourists, but this guy seemed to be a little more bizarre than most. He looked like heatstroke was just a few labored breaths away. They walked over to him and one of the guards gave him a bottle of water.

"Drink up," he said.

Just as the guard was about to ask where in Texas the stranger was from, a silent bullet went through his chin, into his brain and out the back of his head. His body went limp. He fell to the red dirt in front of the shade tree. A light cloud of dust rose into the late afternoon sun.

The other guard reacted admirably, diving to the ground and pulling his pistol, but he was too late. The would-be tourist had killed better men before. Just as the guard hit the dirt, three bullets pierced his torso. A few seconds later, the hit man stood over the lifeless body and put a bullet through his head just to be sure.

He walked across the parking lot to the garage where the handy man was. The hit man was no longer a sweaty, lost and thirsty tourist. He stood tall and took solid, deliberate steps. The friendly slouch of the overweight Texan had transformed into the muscular frame of a professional hit man. His once ill-fitting clothes, now hung smartly. His labored breathing, now calm. His eyes scanned the compound for any movement and entered the garage.

"Yo! Mister, come on out," he said, dropping the Texas accent. "You don't have to die today. All I need you to do is open the door...then you can go home to your family."

Suddenly a shotgun blast blew chunks out of the wall just above his head.

"Damn."

The hit man lay down on the floor and looked under the Mercedes parked in the garage. He took aim and shot the handy man in each ankle. The old man, Uncle Calvin, screamed in pain and went down hard, but he wouldn't let go of his shotgun.

Sliding along the floor, he let off another round taking out the fluorescent lights hanging from the ceiling. He crawled towards the garage door while the hit man made his way around the far side of the car and came up silently behind him. Calvin looked towards the closed-circuit camera as the last bullet went through the back of his head, spraying blood over the polished side panels of the Mongoose's favorite SUV.

Shit, she'll know I'm here now, the hit man thought.

He ran to the steel doors at the main storage tunnel. As expected, they were locked. He took a packet of C-4 out of his fanny pack, set the fuse and stepped to the side and out of range. The door was blown completely off its hinges and clanked noisily to the ground. He knew that he had to act quickly. He had lost the element of surprise. She wouldn't

218

call the cops, but there was a possibility that someone in the area had heard the shotgun or the explosion.

After the dust cleared, he stepped into the storage tunnel. To his delight, lights were brightly illuminating the inside of the Mongoose's lair. He had expected her to cut the lights, as darkness would be to her advantage.

He moved forward slowly, taking note of the arrangement of the furniture and the additional passages towards the back of the storage room. The place reminded him of a World War II era Quonset hut, but without windows. The heat and humidity followed him into the tunnel, but thankfully the air conditioning still hummed and the two hundred feet of earth above him kept the temperature very comfortable.

He passed a tall wooden cabinet and stopped. His instincts told him that she was still in the room. She had not fled down one of the passageways.

Suddenly, the lights went dark.

Temporarily blind, the hit man saw nothing. He froze, ready.

He sensed the razor blade rushing towards his throat. He stepped backward just as it nicked his Adam's apple and a searing pain shot through his left arm. He'd saved his neck, but his left shoulder sustained a deep gash.

He rolled on the cement floor and stopped when he felt the legs of a table. He scooted underneath for protection and reached into his fanny pack. He pulled out a cheap pair of night vision goggles. He had expected the Mongoose to utilize the darkness, but he had underestimated her cleverness. Footsteps disappearing into the bowels of the mountain came to his ears.

He stood up and flexed his left hand. It still worked and he could ignore the pain. He ripped off his Hawaiian shirt and wrapped it around his bloodied shoulder. He moved quickly to the back of the storage room where three passageways branched off in different directions. He listened carefully.

He heard the sound of wind and felt fresh air coming from the tunnel on the right. The other two were still. He followed the fresh air. The tunnel was full of cabinets and shelves. It was being used as originally intended, a cool and dry place to keep valuable commodities. He assumed that these were the Mongoose's ill-gotten treasures. The documents he needed were probably hidden somewhere amongst the piles of boxes. It would take forever to search these caves. He needed the Mongoose. He quickened his pace.

The tunnel narrowed and took a steep incline. He burst forth into the sunshine. He threw off his goggles and blinked in the bright tropical light. The heat and humidity nearly knocked him down. When his eyes adjusted, he realized he was standing inside a grove of eucalyptus trees alongside a golf course fairway. Fresh motorcycle tracks were imprinted on the red earth, heading south towards the main highway.

She was gone.

God dammit, he thought. *Now I'll have to look through everything.*

He turned and went back into the tunnel to begin searching for the jewelry box and the documents so precious to his bosses.

Chapter 39

Lou cursed the evening traffic. He loved the islands, but he hated the roads, the traffic. It seemed like there were more cars than people—especially, heading west at 6:30 PM. Normally, he wouldn't have been caught dead driving during rush-hour. Sadly however, he was on a mission for James—one that he had not entirely agreed to.

"Can't you do something about the traffic?" Lou said to the voice in his head.

"Sorry, it looks like everyone decided to go home at the same time," James said. "Even the side roads are clogged."

"You're not much help."

James had dug extensively into the background and life of Mary Jay Higgins, hoping to find out more about Maggie. She owned a house in Ewa Beach, but when James checked the electricity records, it was easy to see that no one actually lived there. Mary apparently was living off a modest family inheritance—she had no record of employment and paid little in taxes. She spent most of her time volunteering for various local charities that focused on native Hawaiian issues and homelessness.

Maggie, as Mary Jay Higgins, was living in plain sight, but well off anyone's radar. The only interesting thing that James was able to find was that she had been renting an underground storage unit in Waikele for at least ten years.

Lou was on his way to check out the facility.

"Are you sure this is worth our effort?" Lou asked.

"We had this discussion already," James responded.

"I've got lots of time. Let's go over it once more."

"I presume that Maggie cannot live in a storage unit, but clearly this is a place of some importance to her. If you ask around, maybe we can find something."

"And why are we doing this again? Especially since Maggie made it very clear that she wants us to back off," Lou asked.

"We're not looking to interfere, I promise you, but the more we know about Maggie, the better."

"How so?"

"Lou, you want to protect her as much as I do," James said. "Can we end this debate?"

"Okay, but nothing gets documented or transmitted electronically. That means no tips to Morimoto or the HPD, and we only act if we find something that puts Maggie in danger."

"Yes, for the millionth time. Do you want me to make a recording and play it back to you on a continuous loop?"

Lou didn't respond right away. James added, "Relax for a while, you got at least forty-five minutes."

"Thanks for the traffic report, and no thanks to the loop idea."

Lou turned on the radio. The voice in his head went quiet.

He finally pulled into the parking lot of the Waikele Public Storage facility. The sun was setting, the lights in the gulch started to come on. There were only a few people moving boxes and furniture in and out of their units. Some of the storage units were stand-alone steel structures and others, the larger ones, were renovated bunkers accessed by huge steel doors.

He got out of his car and took a deep breath, the air smelled of red dirt and car exhausts. The constant hum of traffic on the highway, and cars flowing into the nearby Waikele Shopping Center added to the gritty central plains ambience.

"The gulch itself runs for miles to the north and south," James said.

222

"Bunkers throughout?"

"Yes, but most privately owned."

"I'm going inside to see what I can find out about our girl Mary Jay Higgins."

"10-4"

Lou turned on all of his local charm while talking to the man and wife who ran the storage facility. He knew James was listening, so he made a special effort to insert as much pidgin and local humor as possible, knowing that it would irritate his partner.

James was not racist or prejudice towards local people, but he was solidly Caucasian and had always felt somewhat disconnected from the local culture. He was uneasy with local dialects and customs. James secretly wished that he could swing through the multicultural landscape of the islands as easily as Lou could. He envied his friend's easy ways.

Lou knew that, and enjoyed rubbing it in. He laughed and joked with the local Japanese couple and soon had them opening up to him as if he were a second son who had just returned from a long absence. After several cups of hot tea, *manju*[34] and rice crackers, he emerged from the main office.

"Nice work!" James said.

Lou hopped into his car before answering.

"No problem braddah, not bad for an ex-Marine."

He drove the car to the far end of the storage facility, went through the side gate and followed the dirt road further into the gulch.

The lovely couple had divulged that Mary Jay Higgins rented a few of their storage units, but more often than not, she would bypass their facility and travel further up into the gulch. They never asked, but they assumed that she

---

[34] Japanese snack made with sweet bean paste

had her own private storage facility somewhere just below Royal Kunia golf course and subdivision.

Lou got the impression that over the years, the couple had received sizable bonuses from Mary Jay Higgins to keep this information confidential. However, Lou's undeniable charm and his very believable stories about their days as childhood friends had loosened their tongues.

The ravine was darker than the surrounding central plains. There were no street lamps along the road. The only illumination came from the occasional naked light bulb hanging above the entrance to one of the storage tunnels. The ambient light from the adjacent subdivisions did not reach to the floor of the Waikele Gulch. There were no other cars. His headlights barely penetrated the dusty darkness. Lou struggled to stay on the narrow road.

James saw the open gate and the two bodies lying in the dirt before Lou did—he had the benefit of telescoped infrared vision. His heart skipped several beats, his stomach scrunched up into a tight ball. He had trouble breathing. He couldn't speak.

Lou slammed on the brakes.

"What the fuck?" Lou said. "Didn't you see them? Are you sleeping?"

"Sorry Lou," James said, struggling for breath. His ventilator alarm beeped.

"Mister Spencer, I be right there," Lillian said through the intercom.

"It's okay, Lillian. I'm fine," he said.

"I'm sure as hell not fine," Lou said.

Lou grabbed his high beam flashlight and got out of the car. The two men were definitely dead. Both had bullets through their heads. Pieces of skull and brain were scattered about. Pools of dark red blood had been absorbed into the dry red dirt. Flies and foraging creatures of all kinds covered the bodies, sucking up whatever moisture and nutrition they could. He heard a lizard or rat scurry into the nearby bushes.

"How long? How long have they been dead?" Lou asked.

"Body temperature indicates several hours, they're stone cold."

"Do we call the cops now, or later?"

"That's your call, you're on the scene," James responded.

Lou swung his flashlight through the hard-packed gravel and dirt yard in front of the storage units. He saw that the doors of one of the bunkers had been blown off. He decided to take a quick look before calling HPD.

"God I hope she got away," Lou said. "I'm going in."

"Roger, I'm with you."

"This was a professional job. Probably the same guy who offed Jefferson and Lin. We might be too late," Lou said.

James stayed silent. He just watched and listened as Lou moved forward. He kept all of his systems at one hundred percent capacity. He made sure every detail was being recorded and analyzed. He was focused, totally immersed in the experience.

Lou drew his pistol and entered the cave.

A few minutes later, Lou reported. "Lots of blood on the floor. No bodies so far."

"Check the wall on the far right, your two o'clock. Looks like there might be a light switch."

A few seconds later, the entire tunnel was flooded with light.

"Welcome to the Mongoose's lair," Lou said.

Chapter 40

Maggie had flown down the back roads of Waipahu on her Kawasaki motorcycle. The vibrations of the 250cc bike masked her shaking body, her sobs. The wind in her face evaporated the wellspring of tears flowing down her cheeks.

The image of Uncle Calvin looking up at the camera and telling her to run just before the Caucasian man blew his brains out, would never leave her. She hadn't seen her guards, but she knew they were dead. They would've never let the hit man get that close without giving up their lives.

It's my fault...

Calvin wouldn't see his grandchildren again. The other men left behind mothers, fathers, siblings and girlfriends. She was grief stricken, angry and scared. She had not anticipated such a bold and direct attack. Campbell and Kobayashi were much more motivated than she'd expected. The hit man was a professional.

She could still feel the way the man's flesh opened to her razor blade. Oddly, the memory of it calmed her nerves. She'd been in tight spots before, and survived a few scuffles, but this was the first time she had drawn real blood. Spatter stained the front of her T-shirt and blue jeans. She was glad the blood was not hers, but regretted the fact that she'd missed his throat. She vowed that if she got a second chance her blade would hit its mark.

She pulled into the driveway of the small beach house and turned off the engine. It was instantly quiet. The only sound she heard in the Ewa Beach community were the waves breaking in the distance and the neighbor's television. She rolled the motorcycle into some hibiscus bushes on the side of the house and made her way to the front porch.

This was her residence, but she had only visited here as Mary Jay Higgins. Tonight, as the Mongoose, to avoid the eyes of curious neighbors she stayed in the shadows. The door key was under the clay pot just where she had left it several weeks ago. She noticed the plants were in need of some care. The house, however, was in good shape.

She made a quick sweep of the entire place, just to make sure no one had let themselves in uninvited. When she was satisfied that she was alone, she stripped off her clothes and took a long hot shower. Tears and red dirt mixed with the water, washing her sorrow down the drain.

I will take care of their families. Uncle Calvin will not be forgotten...

"How did they find me?" She asked.

No answer came from the shower stall walls.

After her shower, Maggie sat down in a large comfortable leather chair facing the ocean. She robotically drank some hot tea and munched on some salty crackers. She looked out over the peaceful scene. The grass on the sand dunes waved at the stars. The white crests of incoming surf reflected the light from the half moon. She pushed the sadness and loss from her heart. She weighed her options.

They were not good.

If Campbell and Kobayashi had found her hideout, they would no doubt find this little house. Going to the farm was out of the question, they would have someone watching all of her relatives. She had to hide somewhere unexpected. She knew that they would never stop looking for her.

Maggie worried that perhaps her family on the farm, her mother, even James and Lou may also be in danger. She opened up the leather satchel that she had managed to grab on her way out of the tunnel. She looked through the documents outlining the construction accident and the subsequent cover-up. She read through the names of the wealthy and powerful local dignitaries that were implicated.

This is my leverage.

She thought about her father and the day she found out he would not be coming home from work. She remembered the deep friendship Uncle Calvin and he had shared. Her sadness took her to Jackass Ginger Falls. She saw Luke being taken away in the ambulance. She remembered crying and pushing everyone away. Memories of her mother's perfume as she lay in the psychiatric ward at Queen's Medical Center came to her. The fragrance was Ginger, her mother's favorite. The raw emotions that surfaced were rooted in anger and revenge. She'd been here before. She knew the dangers of spiraling out of control into darkness. She made a conscious effort to breathe deeply and recall positive memories.

Her eyes watered when she thought about the happy days of her childhood hiking through the forests of Oahu with Luke and her father. His love of the land was paramount, but his love and devotion to his family was even greater. She still felt that love.

She reviewed the lessons her mother had taught her in their cluttered kitchen. Her cooking was always so *ono*—her advice always nonjudgmental and right-on. Maggie heard the songs that her Uncle Calvin and his friends played at their frequent family gatherings. She remembered how being part of the Kawanakapili 'Ohana had calmed her soul. How the bosom of the family had saved her from a life of addiction, and returned joy to her heart.

Memories of the happy carefree years, when she was a teenager, flooded back to her. Images of Lou, James and the rest of the boys running through the forest or driving up the Pali flashed past her eyes. Late nights on Tantalus, necking with Lou, or simply drinking a beer or smoking a joint with her best friends was all the nourishment she needed at the time. Those were good years, she felt safe with her pack.

Will I ever feel safe like that again?

Maggie's slight smile turned serious when she reminisced about the first few years of her life as the Mongoose. She remembered the genuine satisfaction of a successful burglary and a large payout. Saving the farm had been her primary objective, but she found the adrenaline of planning and executing the burglaries to be addictive. She couldn't stop.

Taking revenge on the powerful and wealthy families, making them feel unsafe in their cloistered worlds brought a sense of equilibrium to her. It felt right to live on the border between good and evil. Punishing them was reward enough, but seeing the happy faces of the hard-working not-for-profit volunteers and employees when their charities received large anonymous donations filled her with warmth.

Things are different now. The Mongoose has run her course.

Maggie knew what she had to do.

Chapter 41

The next morning when Maggie, disguised as Mary Jay Higgins, buzzed the condominium intercom, Lillian was not sure if she should let her in. The slightly chubby blonde haired woman was unfamiliar to her. Mister Spencer rarely had unannounced visitors.

The plain clothed detective in the black SUV parked across the street paid little attention to the woman as she got out of the taxicab and walked up to the front door of the condominium, but he took the requisite pictures anyway. His orders were to document all females entering and leaving the building.

She didn't fit the profile. According to Morimoto, they were looking for a small, slender, mid-40s, Hawaiian-Asian woman. Instead of downloading the photos immediately and transmitting them to the precinct server, he decided to wait until he had a larger batch of suspects.

"Mister Spencer," Lillian called to the back room. "Mary Jay Higgins is here to see you."

James quickly switched to the camera at the front door. Maggie looked up at him through her white makeup and blonde wig, he recognized her immediately.

"Come on up!"

"Lillian, please prepare some hot tea and snacks. We have a guest," James said. "And you better wake up Lou." James was thrilled to see Maggie alive.

Lou had arrived at the apartment very late last night. It had taken several hours before detective Morimoto and the HPD released him from the scene. They had talked for a while, and outwardly hoped that Maggie had escaped. There were signs of a struggle and lots of blood, but her body had not been found. Inwardly however, they both had their doubts. It was possible that the hit man had abducted her.

A few minutes later Lillian escorted Maggie into the room. James' caregiver hung protectively by his bedside, while the guest stood awkwardly by the door.

"It's been a very long time," James said.

Maggie just nodded her head, it seemed like the words were there, but her vocal cords would not work.

"It's okay, take a look around. I'm in no pain," he said. "Quite comfortable really, thanks to Lillian."

James was aware that the initial shock of seeing an old friend hooked up to a heart monitor and a ventilator took a while to sink in. He knew that all of the tables, computer equipment, monitors, wires and the LED lights covering the floor, walls and ceiling made for a weird setting. He was patient and tried to reassure her.

"Come in, come closer to the bed."

"Can you move?" She asked.

"Only from the neck up," James said.

Maggie looked cautiously around the room, and then moved closer to the bed.

"Lillian, we will be fine. This is Maggie, one of my best friends from high school. We've got a lot to catch up on."

Lillian took her cue and left them alone.

"Call me if you need anything, Mister Spencer."

A minute later, Lou came storming into the room, grabbed Maggie around the waist and lifted her off the floor. He gave her a sloppy kiss on the cheek, and then dropped her gently, slightly embarrassed with his exuberant display. He smiled, and continued without missing a beat.

"That one's for James. This one is for me!" He said as he grabbed her again, giving her a huge bear hug.

"Lou!" Maggie shouted after the second embrace. "Goodbye Mary Jay Higgins," she said, as she pulled the blonde wig off and shook her shiny black hair until it fell comfortably around her shoulders.

"It's good to see you boys."

"Maggie, I'm so glad you're alive," James said. "You're safe here."

"We want to help," Lou said.

Over the next hour, Maggie told her friends about her escape from the hit man, the involvement of Campbell and Kobayashi, and the documents. She believed that the hit man was a professional, and that he would not stop until the job was done. He was after the documents. Maggie feared that he would use her family, James or Lou to get to her. They were all in danger.

"For the first time in twenty years, I feel lost. I don't know what to do," Maggie said. "I'm sorry I came here dumping my problems on you."

"No worries," Lou said. "We'll figure something out."

"Why don't you relax for a while," James said. "We all need some time to think about this."

"Good idea, I brought some extra clothes. I could use a shower to wash off the rest of Mary Jay," she said, indicating her makeup. Then she reached into her duffel bag. "These are the documents. You might be interested in looking at them."

Maggie gave Lou another hug and James a careful kiss on the cheek.

"Lillian will get you whatever you need."

"Thanks again," she said, and then she left the room.

The two men stared at each other in silence. The vibrant synergy Maggie had brought with her into the room was gone, but a slight hint of Ginger remained. Without speaking, they agreed that this was the right thing to do.

"Lou, can you run the documents through the scanner? I'd like to take a quick look at them, also probably a good idea to have a backup copy."

"What's the plan?" Lou asked.

"I don't know yet, what do you think?"

"I say we throw some bait out there, hook a hit man and filet him."

"Sounds like fun, but it won't solve the long-term problem," James said. "Let me read these documents. There may be some leverage here."

Later, when Maggie had regained her slender figure and natural coffee-colored skin, Lillian served them a delicious lunch. Maggie and Lou enjoyed huge helpings of kimchi fried rice, while James looked on enviously sipping his nutrition shake. They talked about old times. Maggie told them about her life as the Mongoose. The atmosphere felt energized, as if they were teenagers once again.

"Eventually, they will come here," Lou finally said.

"I can leave," Maggie said.

"No way," Lou said. "I can take care of any scum that come this way."

"I can handle myself," Maggie said.

"But, I do think we should let Lillian go for a while," Lou added, looking at James.

"Yes, Lillian deserves a few days off," James said. "At least until this blows over. I'll talk to her. She can show you guys what I need, and we can always call Pablo."

"Okay then, it's settled, we let them come."

"They won't stop until they have the documents," Maggie said. "...and me."

"Maggie's right, we need a more permanent solution," James said.

The three spent the rest of the afternoon and most of the evening pouring through the documents in detail. James and Lou were surprised at the depth of negligence implicated in the Bishop Towers accident.

The construction company, Kobayashi Incorporated, had been cutting corners under pressure from the developers and other investors. Human bones had been found at the site and had gone unreported. There was a rush to lay the foundation and complete the job as quickly as possible—before the discovery was leaked to the press and state archaeologists got involved. A court-mandated survey could delay the project for months or even years. Hundreds of millions of dollars were at stake. The comprehensive nature of the cover-up and the wide net of government officials, politicians and top business executives involved was impressive.

James believed that there was enough evidence in the documents to put many of Honolulu's most powerful and wealthy patriarchs behind bars for a long time. It would shake the city to its core. He thought legal action was the right strategy. For her cooperation, Maggie could possibly arrange a deal for a light or suspended sentence, even immunity.

That evening after discussing his plan with Maggie and Lou, he contacted his most trusted attorney to get the process started. Then, in the morning, he would call Detective Morimoto.

Chapter 42

Detective Morimoto arrived at his office uncharacteristically early. Even though he'd spent most of the previous day and night at the dusty Waikele Gulch crime scene, Morimoto still looked fresh, energetic and well groomed.

I haven't had a day like this for years, he thought. *About fuckin' time.*

His Armani suit slid comfortably into the leather chair behind his uncluttered desk. He sipped his black gourmet coffee and smoked his e-cigarette with great satisfaction. He admired the perfect shine of his shoes and then began flipping through the photographs of the females sent to him by his man stationed outside of Spencer's condominium. Everything was proceeding very nicely. The Mongoose's lair had been discovered, and with the evidence the CSI's were uncovering she would be caught soon enough. This was an island after all—there were few places to hide.

Yes, the Mongoose was a *she.* Her real identity had been surprisingly easy to find among the documents and photographs in the living quarters of the compound—Mae-Linh Malia Nguyen Kawanakapili—a petty thief, prostitute, drug addict, that had dropped off the radar a few years after serving time at WCCC. The MO would reveal itself soon. The Big-Five families would be grateful to have this weasel out of their lives. He was expecting well-deserved praise from the Police Chief and Commissioner.

The Mayor may even call.

There was a knock on his door. He straightened his posture, turned off his cigarette.

"Please, come in," Detective Morimoto said. He surprised himself with the polite tone of his voice and the fact that the word *'please'* had breached his lips, something that had not happened at work for years.

"Boss, I got the DMV database results," one of his rookie cops said.

"24-fuckin' hours," Morimoto's mood soured as soon as he saw the young kid. "What took ya so long?"

"Well sir, I—"

"Forget it, just put the damn thing on my desk and get the hell out of here."

Useless grunt. We already ID'd the Mongoose, running her fingerprints was a waste of time.

Morimoto went back to looking at the photographs. They were his best lead at the moment, but he wasn't focused on the task. He was really just biding his time until the Police Chief called to congratulate him.

Lots of good-looking MILFs[35] in Spencer's neighborhood. Maybe after my promotion I'll move to Nuuanu.

Morimoto tossed the photographs aside. He reviewed Costelilia's statement given at the scene. Spencer's man had been especially tightlipped and borderline uncooperative, so he had held him longer than needed. The story that he had stumbled upon the crime scene after getting lost on his way to a dinner at the Waikele golf course was complete BS. Costelilia was no tourist. Then, after some checking he'd found out that Costelilia, Spencer and Kawanakapili were high school chums, the pieces fell into place. That by itself was enough to justify the surveillance on Spencer's apartment.

The question was why. Why were they looking for the Mongoose? Were they working together?

She just might show up at Spencer's place.

---

[35] Mother I'd Like to Fuck, saying made popular by the movie American Pie

He put the report down and glanced at the DMV report. Two names were listed—Kawanakapili and someone named Mary Jay Higgins.

Why hadn't the stupid rookie said something...total incompetence.

The Mongoose had an alias.

Morimoto pulled up her photograph and stats from the DMV database—Caucasian, blonde, blue eyes, 5'5", medium built, 135 pounds. He immediately went back to the photographs from the condominium.

There she is. She arrived at Spencer's place yesterday morning. Clever disguise... I've got them.

Suddenly, his phone rang.

The Chief, no doubt, he thought.

"Yes sir," he answered without looking at the caller ID.

"Detective Morimoto?"

At first, he was disappointed not hearing the Police Chief's voice, but then he realized it was Doctor Spencer.

"Hello Doctor," he said, sounding almost jovial. "I'm glad you called."

How convenient, everything is going my way, he marveled.

Chapter 43

Walter Kobayashi hated to make these types of phone calls, especially with Campbell sitting next to him. He wiped his perpetually foggy glasses again and peered into his little black book of contacts. Campbell fidgeted with the silverware on the table, irritated with his friend's slow pace. He waved the waiter out of the small private room. It was still early in the day—the Pacific Club was just beginning to welcome the mid-morning breakfast clientele.

The previous call with detective Morimoto had gone quite well. The detective was still on their payroll, although they rarely used his services. Collecting the particular documents from the Mongoose before he made his arrest was a simple task, made all the more possible considering that the detective knew where she was hiding—Spencer's apartment. He had balked at first when Kobayashi ordered him to coordinate with the other man, but an extra bonus was all it took to convince the detective to do their bidding. All he had to do was retrieve the documents—the other man would do the rest.

Kobayashi began to dial the hit man's burner phone.

"Be clear with your instructions," Campbell said. "No loose ends."

Kobayashi nodded that he understood.

The call was short and direct. The hit man knew he had failed the first time, so getting this second chance was unexpected. He accepted the contract and payment terms quickly and without negotiation. He assured Kobayashi that he would succeed this time, and that all of the necessary loose ends—the Mongoose, Spencer and Costelilia—would be packaged neatly. Not having to deal with the documents made the job easier.

Afterward the calls, Campbell ordered fresh coffee and some light pastries. The two men were satisfied that this ordeal would soon be over. They now had two resources in play. They knew where the Mongoose was, and with the right incentive, she would most certainly turn over the documents. All their bases were covered. They relaxed knowing that one or the other would be successful.

Chapter 44

The next morning, Lou let detective Morimoto into the apartment. Lillian had been happy to take a short vacation to visit her sister on the Big Island.

"Where is she?" Morimoto asked, looking around the apartment.

"She's in a safe location until all this blows over," Lou said. "James is in the back bedroom."

"That wasn't the deal," Morimoto said.

"Well, it is now," Lou replied, leading the way to James' room. "Not even a thank you for bringing you to the Mongoose's lair."

"Yeah, thanks a lot," Morimoto said. "Lots of good loot for the CSI's to sift through. Some of the old families will be happy to have their stuff back."

"You're welcome." Lou could tell the detective was not sincere, neither was he.

"So you guys knew about the Mongoose all along?"

"You have to ask James that question."

Lou opened the door.

"Detective Morimoto, thank you so much for coming," James said.

Without moving deeper into the room, detective Morimoto said, "Look, Spencer, our deal was for you to turn over the Mongoose, Kawanakapili, Mary Jay Higgins, whatever the hell her name is...and I review the documents. If they are as valuable as you say they are, then we would talk about a deal with the DA."

"Just a slight change," James said. "Sit down detective. Please take a look at the documents—I'm sure that in just a few minutes you'll understand our reluctance to turn over Mary Jay Higgins to you."

This is just too easy, Morimoto thought, but he decided to keep up the perturbed cop front.

"No, I don't understand. What does she mean to you guys? How long have you known the identity of the Mongoose?"

"She's an old friend, someone we would like to help if we can," Lou said.

"You're harboring a fugitive, and close to obstructing justice—you understand that, don't you?"

"We understand," Lou replied, handing the detective a binder full of documents.

"Now read," James said. "Lou can bring you some coffee."

"No thanks."

Morimoto sat down at a small table and began to glance through the papers, every once in a while stopping to read more carefully or make a comment to himself. James continued to analyze the information on his computer screen. Many of the entries for persons who had received bribes were identified only with initials or job titles. It would take some time to figure out exactly who they all were, but with his unprecedented database access and the algorithm he had written late last night he was beginning to make progress. Lou fidgeted uncomfortably in the corner of the room.

"Lou, I would sure enjoy some cold water," James said, coming to his rescue.

"Sure, great idea. Dave do you want something?"

"Well, yeah I guess that coffee sounds good. I don't suppose I can smoke in here?" Morimoto replied, surprised that Costelilia knew his first name.

"No, please don't detective," James said. "Any kind of particles in the air can disturb my breathing."

Lou looked at James to be sure he was okay, and then left the room for the kitchen.

"Okay, I'm almost done anyhow. I think I've seen enough."

More than enough, Morimoto thought. *A few more minutes of this charade, play it cool. Gain their trust. I need to find out where the copies are and destroy them. The other man should be here very soon.*

"Did I just hear Lou call you Dave?" James asked.

"Yep, David William Morimoto at your service," he replied.

"I like Detective Morimoto better," James said.

"Same here," the detective replied. "Does Costelilia call everyone by their first name?"

"Yeah, a hobby of his."

James switched off his voice recognition–dictation software and maximized the eye gaze system. It allowed him to control his computer systems without using his voice. He wanted to search the documents and possibly communicate with Maggie and Lou by text without alerting the detective. His gut told him that something was very wrong.

The initials DWM had triggered some synapses in the area of his brain that processed short-term memory into useful data. He flipped through the documents listing persons that had received bribes. There it was, DWM a Building Permits and Inspection Officer with the Honolulu City Office of Development and Planning had received a series of $10,000 payments from 1971 until 1974. A quick check of Morimoto's curriculum vitae showed that he had graduated from the University of Hawaii with a degree in civil engineering in 1970. His first job was with the city government.

"How long have you been with the HPD?" James asked, pretending to keep up the friendly chitchat.

"Almost thirty years now, time to retire."

"I hear you," James said.

James sent a text message to Lou and Maggie, laboriously picking out each letter and word from a pop-up menu. He prayed that Lou would check his cell phone. He knew that Maggie was watching and listening from the safe room. The text message would appear on her monitor.

DWM is on the list of payoffs! Use extreme caution.

Lou heard his phone beep. It was on the coffee table next to the couch where he had spent the night. He wasn't expecting any important phone calls or messages, so he let it go. Instead, he brought the coffee and water to the bedroom.

Morimoto was still reading through the documents. He took the coffee graciously and continued his investigation. He took a few notes. He glanced at his watch. The detective's left leg shook nervously as if he was waiting for something.

James took a quick sip of the cold water proffered by Lou and then looked him directly in the eyes.

"I heard your cell phone," James said.

"Yeah, you and your acute sense of hearing," Lou said. "Nothing to worry about."

"I think you better answer, it might be Lillian or the Governor's office."

Lou looked at James with a perturbed expression. James never paid any attention to his telephone calls before.

James glared at him. His eyes said it all.

Lou excused himself, went to the back bedroom, and retrieved his Glock. He made sure the clip was full and the safety was off, and then he checked the text message on his phone.

"The bastard," Lou whispered to himself.

He stormed into the bedroom to find Morimoto standing over James with his pistol pointed at his left temple.

"Put the weapon down, Costelilia. Any sudden moves and your friend is dead."

246

Lou threw his gun on the bed within reach of James.

"Nice try, but I know your friend here can't move a muscle," Morimoto said. "Now sit down quietly while Doctor Spencer and I have a chat."

Lou did as he was told.

"Good, now like I said Spencer, show me the copies of the documents on your computer and let's delete them— let's make sure we get all of them. Then, we can talk about the location of the Mongoose."

Chapter 45

Horrified, Maggie watched everything from the monitors in the safe room just off the kitchen. Seconds after she received the text message from James, the detective had gotten out of his chair and pulled his gun. When Lou entered the bedroom with his pistol drawn, she had begged him to shoot, but the detective was smart, he stayed low and close to James' torso. They both knew that if Lou started firing the chances of James surviving were slim. Lou did what he had to do. He tossed his Glock on to the bed and took a seat in the chair by the door.

Another text message popped up on the monitor. James was still able to manipulate his computer without talking.

Stay in the safe room. We will be all right. Call 911.

Just then, an alarm went off in the apartment. She looked at a second computer monitor and saw that a man had jumped from the roof on to the Leeward porch. The motion sensors had picked him up. She heard detective Morimoto giving James some orders.

"Turn off the damn alarm. Don't do anything stupid. All I want is the documents and the location of the girl."

"Okay, okay," James said. "Take it easy. It's just a proximity alarm on the porch, probably a bird or the neighbor's cat."

James looked at the video on a second monitor across the room. *This looks to be our hit man, gotta do something quick.*

Morimoto followed his eyes to the monitor. "Don't play games, we both know who it is..."

"You bastard, you won't get away with this," Lou said, also noticing the man on the monitor, now moving through the apartment. "You better kill me now."

"Don't tempt me," Morimoto said, waving his gun. "But I suppose the pleasure will be someone else's." Then he turned his attention back to James.

"Now, the files..."

Maggie watched the Caucasian man move carefully across the living room. She recognized him. It was the hit man. This was the man who had killed Uncle Calvin, her security guards, and probably Jefferson and Chinn Ho. Last time he had nearly gotten her. She knew that this time he was here for all of them. He was here to finish the job. There was no time to call 911.

I have to do something now.

She grabbed her razor blade from the bottom of her duffel bag and slipped out of the safe room.

As the man walked down the hallway to James' room, she slid in behind him. Her Chinatown gang training and the years she had wielded the custom razor blade as the Mongoose came to the forefront. She held the weapon firmly and with purpose. She got closer, then instinctively, she jumped off the floor just high enough so that her right arm and right hand that held the razor blade were level with the man's throat. She wasn't going to miss this time.

With her left hand, she grabbed the man's hair and pulled his head slightly back. Her blade sliced cleanly through his Adam's apple. His body went limp as he dropped his gun and reached for his throat. Blood gushed in all directions. She held on to his back as he thrashed about, and then took his last gasping breath. He crashed to the floor, dead.

She fell on top of him with a loud thump, and then there was silence.

I've done it. Is this what revenge feels like?

She heard a large bang, screams and a scuffle in the bedroom.

Chapter 46

James was aware that his steel framed lift was just behind his head where it was usually stored. While Morimoto's attention was focused on Lou and the alarm, James activated the lift with his eyes.

He set the power to full.

"Morimoto, you don't have to do this," he whispered, trying to draw him closer. "We can destroy the documents or remove your discretions."

Morimoto leaned in to hear the bedridden man's words.

"It's too late," the detective replied. "You'll be better off dead."

I'm not ready to go yet, James thought as he flashed his eyes across the screen, activating the lift. The heavy metal frame slammed into Morimoto's head just as he was straightening up.

Lou sprang into action, leaping over the bed and crashing the older man into the wall. The detective's gun went flying. Lou applied maximum force to the man's most vulnerable pressure point, just below the sternum. Morimoto screamed in agony. Lou pushed harder until the man went unconscious, and then he punched him in the face a few times.

It was over in seconds. Morimoto was lying in a heap on the floor. Lou stood over him breathing heavily.

"Yes!" James yelled.

Lou quickly retrieved his Glock off the bed, turned, and was poised to fire when Maggie ran into the room.

She stopped and froze.

"Where's the other guy?" Lou asked.

"Dead."

"Are you all right?"

She was covered in blood.

"I'm fine. It's not mine."

Lou touched James' legs as he passed the bed and moved over to where Maggie stood. He embraced her, tentatively. She accepted the gesture unconditionally.

She dropped the razor blade and began to sob.

Lou looked over her shoulder at James. "Jimmy, you okay?"

"Yeah...Is he dead?" He asked, glancing to the side of his bed in Morimoto's direction.

"No, but he'll be out for while," Lou answered. "I'll tie him up in a minute."

The room was quiet except for the rhythmic hum of the ventilator and CPUs.

"What now?" Lou finally asked.

"Call the Governor."

Chapter 47

The Hawaiian blessing held in the northern corner of the Bishop Towers main lobby was a small private affair. The Governor had invited just a few of the most important leaders of the Hawaiian and local business community. A couple of the Big-Five families were also represented and some of the Governor's closest political allies.

James could tell that Lou would have preferred to skip the ceremony, but Maggie was happy to be there. For her the gathering was more than just a blessing for the bones of the ancestors buried beneath the building's foundation— this was a long overdue tribute to her father and the other men who had needlessly lost their lives here.

The *Kahuna*[36] and her attendants moved around the roped off section of the lobby chanting and spreading purified water with Tealeaves. James closed his eyes and let the sound of the ceremony wash over him. He felt relieved and relaxed. It had been a busy ten months of negotiations and litigation. The call to the Governor had been the right thing to do. He had immediately created a task force with the District Attorney's office to handle the investigation. The arrest and prosecution of the people implicated in the accident and cover-up went on for several months.

Jonathan Campbell and Walter Kobayashi were indicted for conspiracy to commit murder, bribery, and several other charges. They expected to spend the remainder of their lives in prison. The rest of the Big-Five families escaped relatively unharmed, paying fines or making donations to one of the Governor's pet projects. They agreed to drop the charges against the Mongoose and she helped the families reclaim as many of the heirlooms as possible.

---

[36] Priest

Detective Morimoto faced charges of attempted murder, falsifying documents and accepting bribes. The HPD was shocked to learn that one of their own was "dirty" and on the payroll of the Big-Five. A large and slow-moving internal audit was undertaken throughout all levels of City and State Government agencies. A host of officials were in line to be tried for their role in the cover-up—everything from falsifying documents, extortion, accepting bribes, and perjury.

The chanting stopped. James opened his eyes and listened to the Hawaiian elder.

"My mentor taught me to call upon *Ke Akua*[37] and the spiritual guides associated with the land for which today's blessing is being sought. Our chanting and the blessing of purified water will heal the land."

The kahuna looked around the lobby, "However, in this case, we must do more. We are gathered here to right a wrong and honor the bones of our ancestors who are entombed in the floor below us." She paused.

"To do this I must call upon my own ancestors and the ancestors of the people involved. I ask all of their spirits to join us in prayer. I also call upon those physically present, all of you...to add your *mana* to the blessing. We ask those who are to come after us to watch over this place, and to keep it within their hearts."

James felt Maggie squeeze his hand lightly—*thank you*, the gesture said.

Lou gave him a firm pat on the chest—*'keep breathing buddy.'*

The *kumu*[38] continued, "Past, present, future—that is the way of life and the way of the land. We must remember

---

[37] The Supreme Creator
[38] Master Teacher

that the land was here before us, and will be here after us. We are merely a thread in a long succession of stewards."

Chapter 48

The van pulled into the parking lot at Tantalus lookout. A big, athletic man jumped out of the drivers' side and proceeded to open the double doors in the back. A small, slender Asian woman joined him and pushed the button to lower the ramp. They both reached inside and pulled the wheelchair carrying the handicapped man onto the pavement. The big man pushed the wheelchair to the very end of the of the viewing area. Tourist and locals politely gave way to the threesome.

"Perfect timing," James said to his friends on either side.

The sun had just about fifteen minutes to warm the islands before it would dip below the horizon. The high clouds were a mixture of bright pink and orange. The lower, heavier clouds took on a subdued grayish purple color. Diamondhead reflected the last yellow rays of the setting sun.

To their right, a passenger airliner silently cleared the runway at Honolulu International Airport and banked sharply to the right. The horizon slowly disappeared as the dark blue ocean began to blend with the early evening sky. The curvature of the planet was still clearly discernible, but as darkness took over, the line between the Earth and the Galaxy became less and less defined.

Lou remembered when they had frequented this place as teenagers. It had changed a lot since then, but the view was still the same.

He had changed a lot. Nightmares and nostalgia no longer kept him awake at night. He looked forward to each new day.

"Maggie, I'm sorry about Luke," Lou said.

"It wasn't your fault, Louis," she said. "I know now that it was an accident that none of us could have prevented."

Maggie felt a freedom that she had not felt for more than twenty-five years. When they spread Mary Jay Higgins ashes off Waimanalo beach, and so many people came to pay their respects, Mae-Linh Malia Nguyen Kawanakapili was reborn. Revenge and sadness no longer ruled her heart. Dusk and dawn were no longer her preferred hours of activity.

"Thank you for bringing me out tonight," James said. "It's beautiful."

James was the happiest he had been in many years. He felt centered and very much alive. The terminal nature of his disease no longer played games with his psyche. He had recently begun to invest time and money into developing an implant that featured artificial bio-generated nano-tendrils that could possibly mimic motor neurons. It was no cure, but there was the possibility of bringing some muscular functionality back to people with severe brain injuries or degenerative muscular diseases.

The three friends watched as the Honolulu city lights competed with the stars of the Milky Way. There was no winner in this timeless battle, each sparkling pinpoint of light was the source of its own infinite beauty.

The scent of Ginger lingered on the night air.

Acknowledgments

Many people have helped me with the conception and completion of this novel. I thank all of you, named and unnamed. Without you, your love and support, this therapeutic endeavor of mine would not be possible.

Thanks to my great friend Bob Steen for encouraging me to write a crime story. For those of you that know him and our relationship, it will be easy to see that Lou is loosely based on our friendship.

I also would like to give a shout out to the movie *The Bone Collector* (1999). The idea that a terminally ill bedridden genius could fight crime found some roots in this movie and fertilized my imagination.

During the writing of this novel, I enrolled in an online Fiction Writing Course offered by Gotham Writers Workshop, in New York. The feedback from the instructor and the students on the first few chapters of this book were very valuable and encouraging. I specifically would like to thank Phil Sykora and Oscar Pogarian. Phil read the entire first draft and gave me some excellent suggestions. Oscar read through the final proof, finding some of those elusive typos, grammar and punctuation errors, unnecessary adjectives and awkward sentences.

As an added benefit from this class, I made a close friend, Karen Watson, also a beginning writer. Through cyberspace, and thousands of miles between her home in Montana and my apartment here in Honolulu, we have forged a mutually beneficial collaboration. We have agreed to review each other's work and to give each other critical and honest feedback. I believe that both of us have become better writers through this collaboration. Thank you, Karen.

Thanks go to my caregivers. Josie is the inspiration for Lillian.

Thank you to Andrea and Peggy for reading some of these chapters to me. It's always great to hear my words through someone else's voice. Also, thanks for typing difficult words that my speech recognition software refused to comprehend.

As always, much love goes to my family—my father, my sister, my son and my wife. I love you all.

Rick
January 2014

Other works by R.K. Raker

The Gunslinger's Vision, Volume 3 of the Gunslinger Series, A novella self-published December 2013.

The Gunslinger's Fall, Volume 2 of the Gunslinger Series, a novella self-published September 2013

The Gunslinger's Confession, Volume 1 of the Gunslinger Series, a novella self-published July 2013

Narragansett, a novel self-published June 2013

Not too late for Paradise, a novel self-published March 2013

The Bird-man of Nuuanu Valley, a novella self-published October 2012

The Brookside Rooster, a short story self-published October 2012

The Hamster and the Gecko – A Survivors' Story, a novel self-published August 2012

Sealand 1001, a novel self-published December 2011

A Remarkable Life, lived by an Ordinary Person, an memoir self-published May 2011

Dolphin's Dance, a novel published by PublishAmerica, February 2011

CPSIA information can be obtained at www.ICGtesting.com
Printed in the USA
BVOW06s1116041015

420882BV00019B/331/P